HOLDOUT KILLER

Buchanan slid his hand under his pantleg and got his holdout gun from the top of his boot.

The first hard case saw the movement and started to wheel back but not quickly enough. Buchanan's first shot hit him high in the chest and the second took the top of his head off.

Swinging his gun toward the dead man's pard, Buchanan fired a third shot. The slug knocked the outlaw back, sending him down the rocky washout.

"That was Slater," the deputy said, gasping for air as he clutched his injured arm. "Had a big rep with a gun."

"Well," Buchanan said, "he's got a dead rep now."

BIG SKY REVENGE

JEFF CLINTON

PINNACLE BOOKS
WINDSOR PUBLISHING CORP.

PINNACLE BOOKS

are published by

Windsor Publishing Corp.
475 Park Avenue South
New York, NY 10016

First printing: October, 1991

Printed in the United States of America

PROLOGUE

September, 1863

When Eb Craddock stuck his pick into the mountain and a fortune tumbled out, he should not have been surprised.

Even then, Craddock was no longer a young man by the standards of the harsh frontier where he had lived, man and boy, for more than twenty-five years. He was forty. He thought he had seen everything.

He had come early to the Montana country, had fought the devastating winters while learning to trap with a Frenchman named Jacques, had fought the Frenchman and finally killed him in a knife fight over a canoe of pelts, had hidden from the Nez Percé and fled from the Blackfeet, had been caught once and tortured by Piegans, had spent a winter in a cave with a squaw who was crazy and didn't know who or where she was, had fallen over a precipice near Little Joe Mountain and lived to tell about it, had been shot in the chest once in a fight over a poker hand, had frozen, baked, shivered, sweated, climbed, crawled, waded, rode, staggered, run, fought, stolen, cursed and drunk himself through every valley and over every range and across every river in the goddamned country, and was still broke.

And then he stuck his pick in the mountain here in

the Bitterroot Range, and the results made him feel like his heart had stopped.

Oh, he had heard about the gold strike at Bannack, and he knew the Sapphires were aptly named. But he had never expected anything like this.

Eb Craddock sat down on a boulder, right then and there, and pulled out some whisky and drank it down and thought about what he would have to do to protect what he had found.

The afternoon sky darkened and bitter snowflakes sifted down, the wind moaned through the firs and tamaracks. But Craddock sat there, lost in thought, long after the snowflakes had coated his beaver hat and buffalo coat, making a snowman of him.

Given what he had and what men were, he knew he would have to be very, very clever. He was not going to let somebody steal this from him. He was going to play his cards close to the vest *this* time, and if it took twenty or thirty years for the Indians to be cleaned out of here, and legitimate claims filed by white men, then fine: he could wait.

For this he could wait a hundred years, he thought.

ONE

October, 1877

Outside the cabin, everything was white: the sky like skimmed milk, thin and weakly blue-tinged; the Garnets like glacial ice, all glittering, metallic edges; the Sapphires like rumpled dollops of rich vanilla ice cream. The valley floor—the trees and river canyon and yawning open expanses of field—was coated with silver, and ached the eye.

Inside the cabin, the stone fireplace smoked a little, and that hurt a man's eyes, too.

The old mountain man under the heap of buffalo robes on the rope bed in the corner did not notice the smoke, though. He was busy dying.

At the fireplace, Joe Ford swung the pot of soup off the smoky flames and dipped out a cup of the rich, thick stuff onto a tin plate. Ford was young, twenty-five, tall, blond, lank, with facial lines that betrayed more worry than a man should have packed into his number of years. Lumber boots clomping on the bare plank floor, he carried the soup and spoon from the fireplace to the old man's bed and knelt beside it.

"Come on, Eb," he said gently. "Let's try to eat, here."

Eb Craddock opened rheumy eyes and slowly focused them. He was skin and bones, his slack jaw

7

covered by a wild gray beard that stuck out in all directions. He looked a little crazy. A lot of people said he was crazy, had been for a long time. People had been afraid of old Eb for years, but he wasn't frightening now. He had the sharp smell of death about him.

He licked split, dry lips and whispered so softly the younger man had to bend close to make out the words. "Ain't hongry."

"Dammit, Eb! If you don't eat, how are you going to get better?"

"Dang fool. I'm dying. Anybody could see that. Git outta here. Go back to your own place. Take care of that wife of yours."

"We've been through all that," Joe Ford told him. "You should have come to our place before you got this bad. It was sheer luck I came by yesterday . . . saw no smoke in your chimney. I told you, I'm staying here until you're better. Now sit up and eat this soup, dammit."

"Stubborn idjit," Eb Craddock muttered. But he struggled up on one elbow and let Ford start spooning some of the potato soup into him.

Ford knew it was almost certainly hopeless. He had found the old man unconscious on the floor of the cabin. Eb had been out gallivanting around like a man half his age, and had fallen down the side of a precipice hidden by drifted snow. How he had crawled back to his cabin was a miracle. His left leg was broken. So was his right arm. There were broken ribs that showed purplish through torn flesh. He had vomited three times, and the vomit had bright blood in it.

"You shouldn't have been out in that storm, Eb!"

"Git screwed. I do what I want."

"I'll go for the doctor."

"Doc's in Lolo."

"Somebody can go fetch him."

8

"What for? I'm a dead man. Can't you see that? Are you a idjit?"

"I'll stay with you. The doc will be back in a day or two. I'll go into town then and get him easy. But I'm taking care of you in the meantime."

"You *are* a idjit," Eb Craddock told him then, and violently coughed blood.

That had been yesterday. Joe Ford had left long enough to hike back to his own claim across the sidehill, laboring in through the snow. Margaret had been willing to come back with him, but he had vetoed that. "Stay in. Stay warm. Stay locked up. No one will be out in this weather to bother you. I'll let you know tomorrow how we're doing."

Now Ford was more alarmed than ever. The old man was weakening, sliding away. Ford had never felt so helpless.

He offered Craddock another spoon of soup. Craddock pushed it away, spilling it on the buffalo robes. *"Enough,* goddammit!"

"Eb, you need the strength—"

"Shut up. Shut up." Craddock fell back weakly. "Lemme alone. What are you, some kind of do-gooder? Just because you moved in on the next claim, you got no right to mess in my business. Damn idjit. Git outta here. Lemme alone. I don't need nobody. Think you're gonna git somepin outta me?" He looked up with fierce, crazy suspicion. "Is that it? Is that it? You think you know somepin? Huh?"

"Eb—!" But before Ford could go further, a violent spasm caught in the old man's chest. He hacked wetly, shuddering, his face going red as his eyes bulged and he fought for air. A gout of blood spurted from his mouth and stained his straggly beard and the front of his flannel nightshirt. Ford reached for him to raise his head, but the old man pushed him away.

9

"Lemme alone," he gasped, and fell into unconsciousness.

Ford cleaned him up with a cloth and water from the basin. Craddock's color was even worse, but he seemed to be sleeping. Ford crept to the plank table, sat down on the crate beside it, and ate the rest of the soup.

People in southern Colorado had said he was stupid to come to this country. The summers would bake you and the winters would freeze the remains, they said. The Sioux and the Blackfeet still came through sometimes on raiding parties. The Nez Percé lived on the other side of the Lolo Pass, but they came over here sometimes to hunt . . . and steal. Sure, there was land available on claim from the government. But for what? If nothing else got you, the periodic skirmishes between the cattlemen and the sheepherders might.

Ford had listened and balanced the risk against what he had in Colorado—which was nothing. He'd talked about it with Margaret before they married. Yes, she had said, the most marvelous, gentle, and beautiful woman he had ever imagined, yes; they should go if he wanted it that way, and she would support him.

So they had come to this place not impossibly far from Missoula, had found the piece of land in the foothills and claimed it.

People here had said he was crazy, too—crazy to claim land adjacent to mad old Eb Craddock, one of the real mountain men, a loner who shot at visitors, likely as not, and muttered to himself as he walked along, and sometimes, people said, even talked to bears.

But the land looked fertile and it was the best Ford could locate. He took it.

Eb Craddock had not been hostile. He had simply stayed clear of them for a long time.

Then one afternoon in the late summer, Ford had walked straight into him in the creek bottom that marked part of the boundary between their properties. The old man was wearing skins, a hat made from buffalo hide, homemade boots wrapped with thongs. He saw Ford at the same time Ford saw him, and his ancient buffalo gun came up ready, aimed at Ford's chest.

"Hello!" Ford called nervously. "I'm your neighbor!"

"What you want?" Craddock growled.

"Nothing! Just — hello."

The old man glared for a long moment, then turned and thrashed off into the brush, and vanished.

In the winter, just before the first big snow, Ford had caught a great string of fish. He slung about ten of the fine, fat trout over his shoulder on a long cord and marched across his land to Craddock's, taking care to stay in the open where he could be seen by the suspicious old gent a long way off.

The ugly spang of a bullet going over his head stopped him long before he had Craddock's shack in sight. Craddock lumbered up a long hill, watching him all the way, and Ford stood transfixed, sure that if he moved, the old man would kill him.

Finally they faced each other.

"You're on my land, boy."

"I know."

"Git!"

"I brought you these fish."

Craddock stared. *"Why?"*

"We can't eat them all. We've got plenty salted away."

"Why give 'em to me?"

"Why waste them?"

"What kind of trick is this? Nobody gives me nothing!"

11

It had been a hard day after a hard week after a hard summer. Joe Ford lost his temper. "I don't know why I brought them. I guess I'm weak in the head. Why anybody would try to give something to a suspicious old bastard like you is beyond me. So to hell with you!" And he flung the fish on the ground and turned and walked off.

Four weeks later, Margaret was astonished to find a sack of frozen bear steaks on the front stoop when she opened the cabin door shortly after dawn.

They hadn't exactly been friends since then. But Eb Craddock hadn't shot at him any more.

Now, watching the old man fitfully sleep, Ford wished he wasn't dying. But he knew Craddock was.

There was nothing to do but stay with him, see that he didn't die alone.

Nobody should have to die alone.

Late in the afternoon Craddock roused. Joe Ford, dozing with his back to the brick hearth, started awake at his first movement.

"Water," Craddock choked.

Ford gave him water from the tin cup. Much of it dribbled down the old man's chin and into his beard. He didn't seem to notice.

He leaned back, his color now darker gray, his lips the color of spoiled liver.

"You stuck by me," he whispered.

Leaning close to hear, Ford shook his head. "You're going to get well."

"Got nobody. Got . . . somepin . . . somebody oughtta have."

"Save your breath, old man. After you get well, you'll feel bad if you know you said something friendly."

Craddock moved convulsively. Ford thought for

12

an instant he was starting another coughing fit. But he was only turning to get something out of the covers on the far side.

Turning back, Craddock extended the thing he had retrieved from a hiding place in the bed. It was a piece of soft leather, folded three times into the size of a man's purse.

He held it out to Ford. Ford stared at it.

"Take it," Craddock rasped.

"What is it?"

"*Take* it, you idjit!"

Ford took it. The leather was old, worn, soft in his hands.

"Look at it."

Ford obeyed.

It was a map, worked into the leather with a hot needle, parts colored Indian-fashion with dyes probably applied with the end of a fir twig split and split again with the teeth until it functioned as a brush. Most of the color was faded and gone now, but Ford immediately recognized landmarks—the mountains, the Bitterroot River, the creek that separated his land from Craddock's.

"It's there," Craddock said, pointing to a faint *X* on the map. "See? Under the end of the waterfall."

"What's there?" Ford asked, mystified.

"Dang fool! Ever'thing I stayed here on this land for, all these years. Protecking it. Probably more . . . never found more . . . knew one day I'd find more . . ." A coughing fit stopped him.

Ford stared from him to the map again. "What's out there? You mean you've lived here all these years because something is hidden out there?"

Craddock stopped coughing and nodded violently, his eyes crazy. "Treasure!"

"What?" Ford said, unable to trust his senses. The old man *was* insane after all, he thought.

"Got nobody," Craddock breathed, falling back

13

onto the covers. "No kinfolks. No friends. Had a woman once, but she was crazier'n me. . . ." He seemed to focus his attention with a massive effort, and fixed Ford with those brilliant, crazy eyes. "Be careful! Men would cut your gizzard out for this!"

Then he closed his eyes.

"Eb?" Ford cried, shaking him. "Eb!"

He did not die so easily. In the night Craddock hallucinated, saw deer, elk, coyotes, wolves, bears. He saw Indians, too, and screamed in fear and anger. Ford held him down, tried to talk to him, cleaned up the mess when he was sick again.

At dawn, the old man sat straight up in bed and said, as clearly as anyone had ever said anything, *"Mother?"* And then he fell back and died.

Ford was not sure what to do. He made sure Eb Craddock had no pulse. Then he opened the bottle of whisky on the counter and bolted some down, shuddering. Then he sat a while, trying to figure out his next move.

He felt far worse about the old man's death than he could have expected. It didn't seem right, his dying alone, with no family, no kin. Whatever Craddock had been, he deserved better than that.

When the fire burned low, Ford let it go. After a while, the deep cold began to seep through the cabin. Ford covered the corpse with care, put on his coat and hat, placed the leather map in his inside coat pocket, and left the cabin, closing the door securely.

"You look worn out!" Margaret cried when he clomped into his own cabin an hour later. "I was so worried—Joe! What is it?"

"He's dead," Ford told her. "There was nothing I could do."

With a little murmur, Margaret moved into his arms, snowy coat and all. She was slender and pli-

14

ant and loving, and he held her close for what seemed a long time.

"Who will bury him?" she asked finally.

"I don't know. I'll have to go into town in the morning, tell the marshal."

"Oh, Joe, haven't you done enough? It's so far into town, and this early winter—"

As much as he loved her, Ford felt a burst of anger toward her. "Somebody has to notify the law that he's dead. He didn't have anybody. What do you want me to do? Just leave his body over there in that shack to freeze the rest of the winter and then *rot* next spring?"

Margaret stared, her great eyes widening with shock. "I didn't mean that."

"Oh, hell, honey, I know that," Ford said, instantly contrite.

She hugged him again. "Get out of those wet clothes. I have supper on the fire."

They ate by candlelight as the early darkness crept over the land and the afternoon wind quieted, leaving a vast silence beyond the door. Ford calmed. Margaret was quiet and cautious with him, watching him. He thought how much he loved her, and how grand it would be if the old man's map actually showed the location of something wonderful—a treasure. But that seemed too good to be true, and he did not mention the map to her.

At dawn he saddled the dun and rode into Missoula, its main street a black mud gash in the snow. The sky had cleared and it was bitter cold but windless. Not many people were outside. He found the marshal, a man named Turner, and told him what had happened.

Turner sighed resignedly. "Well, I'll have to go out there, verify how he died."

"Who will bury him?" Ford asked.

"You will," the marshal retorted. Then, as if regretting his bluntness, he added more softly, "Of course I'll help."

The marshal had some other business to take care of before they could leave. Ford went to a saloon and had lunch. He told a few men there about the old mountain man's death. No one seemed much interested.

It was almost dark when Ford and Marshal Turner reached the Craddock cabin. In the light of a bear oil lantern the marshal pulled the hides back off the bed and gave the bluish, stiffened body a cursory examination.

"Took a hell of a fall, all right," he said, standing. "Well, no sense waiting. It's already night, but we got the lantern. Let's plant him."

Under an icy crescent moon they took turns digging in the freezing ground behind the cabin under some old fir trees, on a little hump where the wind would sigh in the boughs and make it nice on summer evenings. They piled rocks on the grave to prevent critters from digging the body up. Then the marshal solemnly shook Ford's hand and settled into the cabin for the night, and Ford went home.

Margaret was waiting for him. His heart gladdened when she opened the door for him. She was tall, blond, with vivid green eyes and lovely features. She murmured gladly in his brief embrace.

Holding her, Ford thought again about the leather map. What if old Eb had really hidden something of value all these years?

He still didn't say anything about it to her because he didn't want to get her hopes up.

But he couldn't get it out of his mind.

Two days later a man rode by with the news that

16

the Indian troubles were over. General Howard had caught Chief Joseph and the Nez Percé up in the Bear Paws somewhere, had a battle, defeated him. Chief Joseph had surrendered and was in custody. So there would be no more threat from the Nez Percé, who had come through the valley recently, scaring a lot of people and stealing horses. And with the Sioux camped up in Redcoat country somewhere, far away and unlikely to risk returning, the immediate area looked to boom with new settlers, new money.

The same day Ford and his wife got this good news, the wind changed to the south and a mild thaw set in, a last respite before the real test of winter.

The next morning, Ford set off alone, telling Margaret he was going hunting. But what he planned to hunt this particular day was not game; it was disclosed on the map concealed in his pocket.

It was a magnificent day: brilliant blue sky, a few low clouds forming a silvery haze on the lower slopes, the upper reaches already blinding white under their winter coat. Crossing a swift stream, its banks encrusted with ice, Ford spooked an elk — a flash of tan and orange — in the long declivity a quarter-mile behind his house, on higher ground. He didn't fire. He saw some deer, a doe and a buck, higher up and at some distance. The light snow under the trees was crisscrossed with the tracks of rabbits, beavers, otters, and skunks. Ford walked steadily, his breath a huge cloud around him, and reached the turning in the creek designated on Craddock's map. He moved on.

By the time he reached the place marked by the X on the map, he was partway up the mountain slope, walking ankle-deep in snow that the sun hadn't melted, spruce and firs studding the landscape around him. There had once been a massive

17

upthrusting of the earthen crust in this region, and slabs of rock stuck out of the ground like giant stone plates crammed one atop another at crazy angles. What had once been horizontal was now almost vertical in the rock formations, and boulders strewn along the hillside attested to other ancient cataclysms he could only speculate about. He had found the blackened pictures of fish skeletons in these rocks, and the tracks of creatures he could not visualize. It was magic country.

The stream at the point where Eb Craddock had marked his *X* on the map was easy to find because of the high rock shelf that overlooked it, more than two thousand feet above. Here the stream sped and shallowed, tumbling over rocks the size of a man's fist, with larger boulders mixed in. The water, over eons, had carved partly through a stone outcropping, making a two-foot waterfall near the earthen bank.

Standing on the side of the stream, Ford stared hard into the cascading water. The sun was precisely in the right position to give him the best possible angle of vision, and he was examining the spot with the keenest expectation of seeing something; otherwise he would never have noticed a thing.

But he did notice something: a duller sheen beneath the thin, rapid-falling sheets of water, a blocky, dark outline that was not natural.

Ford walked over to a nearby dry rock and stuck the rolled leather map under the edge for safekeeping. Then, peeling off his coat, he tossed it over the same rock. He walked back to the edge of the stream and waded in.

The icy water shocked his breath away. The current just below the little waterfall tugged at the lower part of his legs, threatening to push him off balance on the slick round rocks underfoot. Struggling, he leaned over into the jetting water of the

18

fall itself, reached in, ignoring the icy torrent that splattered all over him, and felt for the dull black object hidden behind the water.

His fingers encountered something smooth and metallic. Half-blinded by cold splinters of water, he found a corner of the object, then another, and heaved. It moved. It felt like it was on some kind of natural shelf.

With a lunge he pulled a black metal box out through the concealing waterfall and staggered to the bank with it. He heaved it up onto the mossy mud and stones and climbed out of the stream, dropping to his knees beside it.

It was a metal suitcase or possibly a cashbox, about two feet long and one foot high and deep, very old and very beat up by the water. Once, maybe, it had been shiny. The water had turned it black except around the hasp and hinges, where it was encrusted with dark orange rust.

Eb, what in the hell did you hide here? Ford wondered.

He was really excited now. It occurred to him to drag the box home before trying to open it, but it was extraordinarily heavy for its size, which would make lugging it that far a nuisance. His curiosity was too strong to wait, anyway.

Taking out his hunting knife, he attacked the front lock. The rust had eaten out the lock's innards and it broke open easier than he expected.

Kneeling in the mud and rocks, with the roar of the stream making him oblivious to any other sounds that might have been nearby, Ford opened the lid of the box against the complaint of encrusted back hinges.

The sun peeped through trees nearby just as he did so, and the glow of the reflection off the box's contents lighted his face, almost blinding him.

"My God!" he said.

Transfixed, he did not see the movement out of the trees a few paces away.

He didn't see anything except the contents of the box until the other person's boots tumbled a ball-sized rock down the embankment to splash in the water beside him.

Ford looked up sharply, startled. "What do you want?" he demanded.

Then he saw the black cavern of the revolver muzzle, aimed directly at his face.

Fear gusted as he saw his mistake. He scrambled to get up. It was far too late. He saw the revolver's muzzle flower orange-white, and there was a sharp, imploding pain that almost instantly became softness, and then the light went out.

TWO

April, 1878

The black geld planted its front feet, ducked its head, and pitched Buchanan headfirst into the corral fence. Buchanan hit with stunning impact and lost consciousness for a few seconds.

Then he found himself extracting himself from the boards, the familiar taste of blood in his mouth. The geld was high-kicking across the corral, raising a cloud of yellow dust and chasing the kid helper over the far side and in general being an asshole.

A couple of the waddies working the next enclosure looked over with loud amusement.

"Hey, Jim! You pounding nails with your face?"

"Take it easy on that geld, Jim! I think you plumb got him scared of you!"

Buchanan retrieved his hat, banged it on his thigh, and jammed it back on his head. When he wiped his nose on his gritty bare forearm it left a trail of red.

He walked across the corral toward the geld.

The horse backed away, snorting defiance.

Buchanan caught the reins and jerked the horse around to face him. With the edge of his right hand he chopped down hard on the animal's nose.

The horse staggered backward under the impact and sneezed.

Before the animal could recover, Buchanan moved around it and swung back into the saddle.

The geld went crazy again.

This time Buchanan was ready, not daydreaming.

They went around five times. The other hands stood up to watch. The horse went through its bucking routine, twisting back around on itself, and then stood straight up, trying to throw Buchanan over backwards. When that didn't work, it went around the corral on stiffened legs again, jarring every bone in Buchanan's body.

"Spur him, Jim!"

"Cut him some! Show him who's boss!"

Buchanan hung on, moving with the animal, touching his spurs to its flanks, not to punish, as many horse-breakers did, but only to remind the geld who was in command. He was angry about his earlier carelessness, but you didn't take that out on the horse.

The geld slammed into the fencing, trying to rub him off or break his leg on that side. Buchanan swung his leg over the saddle in self-protection, and then, the moment the horse moved away from the rough boards, got properly seated again.

He could sense the animal's increasing craziness, which was growing in parallel with its diminishing strength. It was a fine animal and it would try—

Without warning, the geld went onto its hind legs again, and then started to topple over backwards to crush its hated burden under its own back.

"Watch 'er, Jim!"

But Buchanan was already out of the saddle

and beside the horse as it crashed over backwards onto its saddle, an enormous cloud of dust whooshing upon all sides. The horse scrambled, kicking wildly, and struggled back to its feet. As it did so, Buchanan swung back into the saddle.

Five minutes later, it was over.

Head down, blowing, the geld responded meekly to the gentle pressure of Buchanan's knees, and walked around the corral as if there had never been any trouble.

Buchanan swung down and led the horse around a few more times, and then turned him over to the kid to cool out and release into the small pasture. The horse was lathered and shaking. Buchanan was a little winded himself.

Walking over to the far fence where the water can hung, he glanced at the Colorado sky. Two more hours until quitting time, maybe three. In the distance, the clouds against the mountains could signal either rain or a late snow.

He reached for the water can.

"Jim?"

Buchanan looked up. The kid was fifteen, scrawny, with carrot-colored hair and a gap in the front of his mouth where some of his teeth should be. He was wearing his bib overalls, his farmer clothes, as usual. He looked pale and upset, so that every freckle stood out.

Buchanan walked over. "Afternoon, Toby. What's going on to bring you out here?"

Toby swallowed hard, his Adam's apple bobbing. His chin stuck out with scared defiance. "I came to say goodbye."

"*Goodbye?* What do you mean?"

"I got to go to Missoula."

"What the hell for?" Buchanan reached out and hugged the kid's shoulders with rough affection.

23

"Hey, I thought we were pals. How come I didn't hear anything about this before? What do you think you have to go clear up there for?"

"It's Joe."

"What's that no-good brother of yours done up there now?"

"I dunno. That's just it."

Buchanan mopped his forearm over his brow. "You want to explain what you're talking about, boy?"

"Something's happened. I know it has."

"Toby, I guess I'm dense. Tell me what you mean."

"I got to go up there because he's bad sick or something and I don't know what and there ain't nobody else to go—"

"Hold it, hold it!" Buchanan put an arm over Toby Ford's shoulders. "Start over. Have you had a letter from your brother with bad news in it, or what?"

"That's just it." The boy's face twisted in worry. "I didn't get no letter in October, so I wrote him again, the fourth or fifth time, and then it got on toward Christmas, and still no letter back, so I wrote some more. And he didn't write to Ma or Pa Snyder, either, and you know how he always wrote to me, and sent them a letter sometimes too, telling 'em how he was getting on, and once he even sent some money, on account of he knows they're poor, and being foster parents to me—"

"But Joe didn't write as usual?"

"No, never. And then he didn't even send me no letter at Christmas, even. But I just kept it to my own self, the worry, I mean. But then last month was my birthday, Jim. My *birthday*. He never, ever forgot my birthday. Something has happened to him, I know it!"

24

Buchanan felt the stirring of a grim feeling that the boy was right. Whatever Joe Ford had or hadn't been, he had been a good big brother to this boy since the death of their real parents a decade earlier. When Joe Ford had left this area, it had been with a solemn promise to stay close in touch, and send for Toby once he was settled on his claim and secure in his future.

But that had been three years ago now. . . .

"There's nobody else to go," Toby told him now. "I got to go find out what's happened."

"You're too young, son."

"What about Margaret?" the boy demanded. "What if something bad has happened to Joe, and she's up there alone, stuck, maybe in awful trouble?"

Buchanan did not answer at once. Behind him somewhere one of the boys whooped as a horse got loose and jumped crazily all over the adjacent corral. Buchanan felt like he was in a cold, isolated space, suspended outside the reality he heard and felt around him.

The mention of Margaret had caught him unprepared, somehow, and hit him like a locomotive. He felt sick, filled with pain and rage, desolate.

The violence of his emotional reaction dismayed him. Wasn't he over all that *yet?* Joe Ford had won. He had lost. Margaret was Joe's wife, and Buchanan was never going to see her again . . . would never hold her close, hurting inside because he loved her so much . . . never see the way the sun made copper-gold shimmers through her hair, or the way her eyes changed as she looked at him, or how her mouth curled, the lips pink and moist —

"Jim?" Toby said, concerned. "You all right?"

Buchanan shook himself. "Sure, kid. Fine."

25

"You looked real funny there for a second!"

"I'm fine," Buchanan lied. He collected himself. "Look, Toby. It would be real silly to head all the way up there just because your bud forgot to write for a few months. What you need to do is send another letter."

"I did," Toby Ford piped. "Look!" He pulled a battered envelope out of his back pocket and handed it over.

Buchanan examined it. The envelope was dirty, wrinkled, frayed on the corners like it had been through many hands, over some rough ground. It was addressed to Joe Ford, General Delivery, Missoula, Montana Ty. On the front, right beside the address, somebody had printed: NOT HERE. RETURN TO SENDER.

Buchanan handed the letter back to Toby. "It could be a stupid mistake."

"He *can't* be dead, Jim. But he must be in bad trouble. Somebody has got to go see. There ain't nobody else."

"Wrong," Buchanan said.

"If he ain't in serious trouble, why—"

"No. I meant you're wrong that nobody else is available to go."

"Who?" Toby blurted. Then his face changed. "Aw, Jim! I can't ast you to do that!"

"You didn't ask," Buchanan said. "I decided for myself."

"But why? My gosh, you and Joe had that falling-out."

"He was my best friend for a long time," Buchanan said, as if that explained everything.

And hell, maybe it did explain the instant decision as well as anything else. He didn't really understand it himself.

Was Joe Ford dead? Buchanan had to know, for

26

his own sake and Toby's too. If Joe was really gone, then a piece of Buchanan's life was gone, too, and he had to know that.

And if something had happened to Margaret, he needed to know that as well. If he never learned what had happened in Montana, he knew he would go to his grave a haunted man . . . a guilty man.

If they needed help, he could help. If they were gone, he could find out how and when, and exorcise the ghosts that walked through his mind every night.

That evening he told the foreman he was quitting. The next morning he collected his pay, drew what little he had saved out of the bank, sold his horse for cash, and bought a train ticket.

He felt like a fool, heading out so fast. But he also, stubbornly, felt like he was doing the right thing even if he didn't quite understand why he felt that way.

Sitting in the coach by a window, he built a cigarette and watched the mountains enlarge through the glass. He hoped to hell his premonition of trouble was inaccurate. He didn't want trouble. He had already had enough of that to last a lifetime.

THREE

Missoula, Buchanan thought, didn't look like much.

Climbing off the stage, he surveyed the scene: a clutter of flimsy buildings, some horses and wagons, streets half dust, half mud. A ramshackle wood bridge, heavy timbers staggered over wood support structures, formed a drooping, irregular span over the river. There were a few two-story buildings along the wide streets, with weedy lots interspersed. He could see out the other end of the busiest street to bare country beyond.

Somebody had planted a huge flower and vegetable garden nearby, and some of the earliest flowers blazed in spring color, adding brilliant blues and yellows to the otherwise monochrome street. There was a crudely painted wood sign reading: Missoula, the Garden City.

In the distance, against the clear, cobalt sky, the mountains were beautiful, wooded and snowy in the higher elevations. The humpy hills directly overlooking the town were barren, with stretches of pale snow high up. the mountains looked ageless.

Missoula looked like it had been built yesterday, Buchanan thought.

No one paid any attention to him as he climbed down and shaded his eyes with a cupped hand for

28

his initial look-see. He was tall and thin, with a width of shoulder hidden by his shapeless gray suit. Only his boots and hat marked him as a waddie, and in this country they were a dime a dozen anyway. His broad features and dark hair were unremarkable, except possibly to discerning women, his vivid blue eyes not obviously keener than most. His single-action Colt and holster, along with his split box of ammunition, were in the battered leather sack slung over his shoulder.

He carried his ruck up Front Street to Higgins, passing a long, one-story mercantile company. Horsemen moved by, stirring dust. A farmer and his two skinny boys carried supplies out of the store to a battered flatbed wagon. The air felt thin and cool, but the sun, out of the clear sky, warmed Buchanan's back.

He found a cheap-looking boardinghouse and went inside. There was a drowsy fat man slumped behind the counter.

"Like a room," Buchanan told him.

The man blinked. "Two bits."

"Fine."

"In advance."

Buchanan paid him and signed the register book. "I wonder if you could tell me where to find the law in this town."

The fat man's eyes narrowed slightly. "Federal? Territory? Military? County?"

"You've got lots of law here."

"Lots of offices. Some ain't filled. Missoula's new. Used to be the town was Hellgate. Over that way. Used to have a murder a week over there." The clerk seemed proud of it.

"I'll take the federal man," Buchanan decided.

"Marshal ain't in town."

29

"Territory, then."

"Ain't no local man."

"County?"

"Sheriff's probably at the jail."

"Where's that?"

"Next to the new courthouse. You walk that-away. Can't miss it."

Buchanan stowed his ruck in the assigned room and then left to look for the courthouse. It was big for Missoula all right, and seemed busy. He found the jail nearby.

It was made of big logs and timbers, with some granite thrown in. There was only one window in front, and it was barred.

The front office inside was dark, a dank and tomblike room with walls that oozed black seepage. The window didn't let in much light. At first glance Buchanan saw only two desks and a cookstove.

"Anybody here?" he called.

A lank man of about thirty, wearing a black coat and pants, a white shirt, and a green eyeshade lumbered into view from the dungeon-like back. "What can I do for you?"

Buchanan introduced himself. The other man said he was Deputy Smith.

"I'm looking for information," Buchanan told him. "Trying to locate a friend of mine. Joe Ford."

"Ford? Only Ford I know is Melvin. Runs the store over on—"

"No. This is Joe Ford. He has a claim off of the Pilgrim Road."

Deputy Smith's long, dull-eyed face changed with remembrance. "Joe Ford. Farmer. Yeah. Say, friend, you've got bad news. That feller died last

30

winter."

Buchanan had been prepared, but it was still a blow. He took it in and kept his voice steady. "How?"

"Don't remember, offhand. Some kind of accident, I think."

Why did he suddenly sense evasion? "Do you have a record?"

"Friend, if we kept records of everybody that comes and goes around here, we wouldn't get anything else done."

"There was a woman."

"Yeah? I wouldn't know anything about that."

"Joe Ford's wife. What happened to her?"

"Don't know. Don't recollect anything about her getting hurt or nothing. She probably went back home, wherever that was. That's what women usually do if their old man dies or runs off."

"Where could I find out if their claim is still being worked?"

Deputy Smith removed his eyeshade and scratched his head. "Well, I suppose over in the land office, but they're about six months behind all the time, and they probably can't tell you a thing."

"Thanks."

"Sorry about your buddy."

"Thanks again."

In the land office, the harried clerks knew nothing about the Ford claim beyond its filing papers and location on the map, which they helpfully pointed out. They looked honestly blank when Buchanan asked if anyone knew how Joe Ford had died, or what had happened to his widow.

31

That night in the saloon adjoining his rooming house, Buchanan nursed a couple of drinks over three hours and listened to the talk. Everybody thought the Missoula Valley was going to boom this summer, with threat of the Nez Percé gone and the Sioux chased across the border into Canada. There was talk of new gold strikes. Rumor said two new mines were going to open before summer ended. The cattle picture looked good, and if they were lucky and got some late-summer rain, the farmers would do fine.

It was getting late when Buchanan struck up a conversation with a couple of drovers who said they worked a spread up in the direction of Kalispell. They were easygoing men with no combative edges, the kind Buchanan had grown up with, and after a while he told them of wanting to find out more about what had happened to Joe Ford, and where Margaret might have gone.

"Out on the Pilgrim Road, you say?" one of them repeated. His name was Kaplan and he had bright, intelligent brown eyes under a shelf of dark hair that grew down almost to his eyebrows, giving him a simian look.

"That's what his letters said, and that's what the map shows."

"Well, then, you might ought to go ask around Pilgrim."

"Pilgrim is a town out there?"

The two waddies grinned at each other.

"More like a bunch of falling-down shacks filled with whisky," the other one, whose name was O'Malley, said.

"Aw, there's a store," Kaplan corrected. "And the post office."

O'Malley leered. "And the whorehouse."

"How far is it out there?" Buchanan asked.

"About eight hours on a good horse. But this time of year the road is pretty good."

"If I went out there, who would I look up to try to get some information? Could either of you give me a name?"

"Well, hell," O'Malley said. "You might's well go to the lord high mokus himself."

"And who would that be?"

"The guy that owns the town! Lucas Pilgrim!"

"Pretty big man?"

"The biggest, buddy. I'll tell you what, a cow don't take a shit out in that part of the country without that it's known to Lucas Pilgrim. If you got any chance of finding out anything about your pal, and he lived out on the Pilgrim Road, then Lucas Pilgrim is the man you need to talk to. He knows—and runs—just about everything out that way."

Buchanan finished his drink. "I'm much obliged." He left the saloon.

In the morning a few clouds, the high kind that threatened a change of weather, had slipped in from the direction of Canada, and the air was distinctly chillier. Buchanan filled up on steak and bread and coffee at the Best Cafe, then checked out of the boardinghouse. Wearing his Levi's, chaps, heavy wool shirt and leather coat, with his Colt strapped on, he lugged his rucksack to a livery barn he had spotted earlier.

"How long you need a mount?" the weasel-eyed operator asked with suspicion.

"Couple days, anyway. Maybe a week."

"Headed out of town, are you?"

"Yes."

The operator put his hands on his hips and looked Buchanan up and down with open insolence. "Where? And why?"

"Are you sure that's your business, mister?"

"Hey, friend. I run a business here. I guess I got a right to know where my rent horse is going to be taken, and what he might be used for."

Buchanan breathed deep and endured it. "Pilgrim."

"Headed to Pilgrim, are you?"

"I just said that."

"Business there?"

"Yes."

"What kind—"

"Look. Do you want to rent a horse, or don't you?"

"All right, all right. No offense intended, friend."

"What's your rental rate?"

The operator quoted a figure that was thievery. Buchanan haggled. The operator came down. Buchanan nodded.

"Show me your horses."

The operator took him out to the corral where a dozen horses moved around in the dust.

"That pale roan is a fine animal," the operator said, uncoiling a rope. "He all right with you?"

Buchanan shook his head. "I'll take the real dark chestnut."

"He's a lot of horse. Kind of unpredictable."

"I like the chest on him. I'll take him."

"Wouldn't do to have him pitch you off out there on the side of a mountain, friend."

"You saddle him, I'll ride him."

The operator had some difficulty catching and

34

saddling the big chestnut. He rolled his eye at Buchanan a few times as if expecting help. Buchanan rolled a smoke and watched; at this rental rate, the livery man could do it alone.

Finally the horse was ready. Watching Buchanan tie his ruck behind the saddle, the operator advised, "Ace High Wagon Yard in Pilgrim is the best place. They know me and my animals. I'd appreciate it if you'd use them if you stay overnight in Pilgrim."

"Much obliged." Buchanan swung gracefully into the saddle with a single strong movement. The bay tried a couple of tricks and got slammed under control for his trouble. When Buchanan rode out of the barn with a touch of fingertips to his hat, the horse was behaving perfectly.

The livery operator watched him ride out of sight around a bend in the street two blocks away.

Then, locking his front doors, he hurried over to the jail, where he found the deputy in the dank front office.

"You know the man you wondered about?" the operator said.

"The one I told you about last night?"

"Yep. Well, he just rented a horse from me. Headed out."

"Where?" the deputy asked with a great show of indifferent preoccupation with the coffee pot.

"Headed for Pilgrim."

"Thanks," the deputy said, his back still half-turned.

The livery operator waited a moment, thinking he might get a thank you or a pat on the back. Getting nothing, he left.

A few minutes later, the deputy walked to a saloon and found a lazy kid he had hired for odd jobs in the past. He gave the kid a note, sealed.

"You ride to Pilgrim," he instructed. "You give this to Lucas Pilgrim *personally.* Understand?"

"What," the kid asked dully, "if he won't see me?"

"Say you got a message from me, and he'll see you. Now get going."

The kid reached for his unfinished beer.

The deputy knocked it out of his hand. "Now, you dumb bastard! That note has to get there ahead of somebody else that's already left. So you leave pronto and you ride hard and you don't rest until the envelope is delivered, savvy?"

The kid stuck the envelope in his pants and hurried out.

The deputy ambled back to work. He was well satisfied with himself. Probably the stranger asking questions was no threat to anyone, he thought. But it never hurt to report everything of interest to Lucas Pilgrim. That was what Pilgrim slipped him an extra fifty dollars a month to do.

And, truth to tell, the deputy—like a lot of other people—was secretly more than a little afraid of Pilgrim. He would have done Pilgrim's bidding for nothing, just to stay on his good side.

FOUR

The dirt road out of Missoula toward Pilgrim was not heavily traveled. After an hour or so, Buchanan found it winding into the foothills of some mountains, then twisting sharply higher along sharp drop-offs toward a high, narrow pass. The air became thinner and chillier. Then the road, little more than a brush-choked indentation wide enough for a wagon, descended again into a high meadow, with more mountains beyond and all view of Missoula's valley cut off.

The rent horse moved along at a strong, steady pace. Buchanan did not push him.

A little after noon, he came to the first cabin, well off the road, identified by wispy wood smoke from a distant chimney. A small, crude sign on a post in the weeds at the edge of the roadway said PALMER. identifying the claim.

Buchanan rode on another thirty minutes or so. Lodgepole pines studded the mountainside below which he rode. Farther on he came to older trees, firs and a few tamaracks. The mountainside was partly denuded on his right, lifting steadily upward to high, craggy granite cliffs perhaps two thousand feet above.

Sticking out of a cluster of ferns growing in a drainage depression beneath some ponderosa pines

37

was another of the claim marker posts. The block-printed sign read FORD.

Buchanan turned his mount off the roadway and moved uphill, following the faint, old depressions in the wooded undergrowth.

Ten minutes later he came out from a stand of spruce and firs to be confronted by a long, sloping meadow with a handful of stumps attesting to someone's previous hard work. At the far end of the hundred-yard meadow, under the shadow of the mountain face, stood a small log cabin.

No smoke came from the chimney, and even at a distance Buchanan could see boards nailed across the front door.

He rode to the cabin, dismounted, tied the chestnut to the hitching post, and walked around the cabin, looking it over.

Some kind of animal had torn the woodpile apart in back. Birds were starting nests in the wooden shingle eaves. Fresh growth of fern and weed had already started to retake the shady rear area that evidently had been trodden bare by footsteps in previous years. Buchanan found a rusty axe leaning against a tree, and a depression where trash had been buried, now open to the faint sunlight after some critter had dug it up, too.

In a vast and windy silence, Buchanan walked to the front of the cabin and confronted the heavy, rough-cut planks nailed crisscross to bar the door. He thought about it. He felt very much alone, and for just an instant he was aware that caution would dictate riding away, taking this as proof that Joe and Margaret were both gone.

Well, the hell with that.

Going back around the cabin he got the axe. Using it as a pry, he peeled the planks off the door with little trouble. Breathing heavily from the exertion at this altitude, he swung the cabin door open and stepped inside.

Mice scurried as light shafted across the dusty floor. The cabin was dark and smelled of winter rot and old woodsmoke. But despite the mess made by the mice on the shelves and cabinet, the interior gave Buchanan a sharp shock.

The covers on the bed were neatly folded back—except where mice had chewed at them—as if just made for the day. Cups and dishes stood neatly on the table, as if someone had just stepped out for a breath of air. There was firewood on the hearth, a cooking pot over the ashes of a fire, a coffeepot on the counter.

A shawl hung draped over the back of a willow rocking chair. Pegs on the far wall held trousers and shirts and coats—and dresses.

The quiet pulsed in Buchanan's ears. He became aware of the distant sound of a brook, and the sigh of wind. He felt like he had been transported into some alien dimension. *What had happened that they had simply vanished?*

A slight sound came from the doorstep behind him. He was so drawn into the eeriness of the situation—finding everything untouched and normal—that he turned with the wild thought that it would be Joe Ford, with Margaret at his side, the rest of this a dream.

The man in the doorway jerked him back to reality.

He was thin, less than five feet tall, and wore filthy cowman's shirt and pants with a ragged derby on his bullet-shaped skull. His face looked like it had been pushed through a funnel, and his eyes gleamed with an intensity such as Buch-

39

anan had once seen on a cornered wolverine.

He had a revolver in his hand that looked much too big for him, but the way he held it was proof that he knew perfectly well how to handle it.

"Don't do anything," the skinny dwarf rasped. "I'd just as soon kill you as look at you."

Buchanan carefully kept his hands above the waist and in the open. "Who are you?"

The dwarf's face twisted into maniacal anger. "Huh-uh! Huh-uh! *I* ask the questions here! Who are *you* and what are you doin' here?"

Buchanan had seen men crazed by various things—the horror of war, the pain of family death, fear of a mob and of Indians, financial ruin, the cruelty of a woman. He had never seen quite the kind of elated cruelty and madness that danced in the little man's eyes. Color splotched his face. His lips twitched, baring yellow teeth like a wild animal's. The man was on a hair trigger.

"Name is Jim Buchanan. I'm a friend of Joe Ford's. I came looking for him."

"Dead. He's dead." The crazy eyes darted around the room. "This ain't his place no more."

"Who does it belong to? And how?"

"None of your goddamn business. Git out. I ought to kill you for trespassin'. Don't never come back. Go!"

Swallowing anger, Buchanan started for the door. He didn't want to tangle with a madman. He could sort out all the questions later.

Unexpectedly the little man moved toward him as he neared the door; his free hand reached toward Buchanan's holster, fingers like claws. "I'll just take your piece to make sure you don't—"

He got no farther because, as much as he might

40

want to avoid trouble, Buchanan couldn't allow that.

With a swift backhand, Buchanan's closed fist slammed into the side of the little man's face. The derby went flying. The dwarf screamed something, but Buchanan had already hammered him up against the door and brought a knee up in his groin, doubling him. The man's Colt hit the floor and slid heavily away. In the same movement Buchanan unholstered his own gun and jammed it up against the little man's mouth, metal grating painfully on teeth.

The dwarf froze, his eyes rolling with sudden terror.

"What's your name?" Buchanan hissed, his face an inch from the other's.

"Shue," the dwarf panted. "George Shue."

"Who do you work for?"

"None of your—" The gun muzzle jammed harder. A tooth broke off with a sharp crack. "All right! All right! Pilgrim! I work for Pilgrim!"

"And you say this is his land claim now?"

"Yeah! Or will be, soon. I was told to watch over the place, don't let nobody mess around it."

Buchanan stepped back a pace, letting him breathe. "I'm on the way to the town of Pilgrim. We'll ride together."

The little man's face became fiendish with rage. "Me? Ride with *you*? I wouldn't be caught dead—"

"I don't cotton to your company any more than you like mine, Shue. But I don't reckon I'll leave you loose out here, so maybe you could sneak up behind me. We'll just ride into Pilgrim together and have a talk with your boss, you and me. That

41

way I can get the answers I need, and you can be sure you did your duty."

"You think I'll ride in there without my gun, and have ever'body know you're *bringing* me in, beat me?"

Buchanan thought about it a moment, then went over and scooped Shue's revolver off the floor. Quickly he punched the bullets out of the chambers and in the same movement tossed the gun. Shue, surprised, caught it anyway.

"You'll have your piece. Put it in your holster. Good. We'll ride in like pals, Shue. No embarrassment for anybody. Meet your approval?"

A crafty look scuttered across the little man's eyes as he holstered his weapon.

"I'll take it real unkind if you try a trick on me," Buchanan added in a voice so soft it was almost inaudible. "I might react real bad if that happened. I'm trying to get along with you, here, and this is the best thing I can figure. But don't try anything on me, Shue. Don't make me lose my temper."

Shue's bright, mad eyes studied him. The instant of silence dragged out. Shue saw something in Buchanan that he perhaps hadn't noticed before.

"I'll . . . be good," he said thickly.

"That's real fine. Now let's nail this front door back shut and head for town."

FIVE

Thin, high clouds had slipped in to obscure the sun by the time they rode into Pilgrim, and the air in the narrow canyon had turned chill. Buchanan kept his horse slightly behind Shue's hammerheaded red roan, watching closely. But the little man's stiff back and erect head were the only signs of what had to be sizzling anger.

The town consisted of about fifteen buildings— a couple of them weather-blackened shacks—along a single narrow street that turned sharply along half its length to go over a log bridge straddling a swift-running creek. A crude grain elevator dominated, standing up against the pines and firs of the mountainside that towered over the town's east side. Buchanan identified two livery barns, three saloons, a general store/post office with a flag in front, a rock building that looked like it should be a bank, a blacksmith's shop, a leatherworker's shack, a couple of rooming houses. Beyond the bridge he could see a cafe sign and what might be a bawdy house.

Three town loafers looked up covertly from a whittler's bench in front of the blacksmith's shop as Buchanan and Shue drifted by, riding easy. One of them left the bench and hightailed down behind the buildings. Carrying the news of their arrival, Buchanan thought.

43

"Where will I find him?" Buchanan asked.

"Big Dollar Saloon," Shue said, tight-lipped. He was angrier, more spring-coiled now that they were in town, where he felt his disgrace.

They rode to the saloon, which was two stories high, with rococo railing around a useless upper balcony. Everything was so quiet they could hear the creek tumbling over big white rocks a half-block away. Buchanan and Shue got down and tied their horses.

A whip-slender man stood leaning against a balcony support pillar. He wore dusty rider's clothes and a floppy-sided Stetson. He looked very young, but the small badge of a lawman gleamed dully on his black vest. Buchanan wondered what kind of law he was, and whose law he was. Not knowing, he ignored the man's open scrutiny and gestured for Shue to enter the saloon ahead of him.

It was dim inside, cavernous, with an open, timbered ceiling, and smelled strongly of sweat, tobacco, whisky, and woodsmoke. An old man lay asleep at one of the front tables, his head on folded arms. At the bar, four younger men stood in a loose group, nursing beers. The bartender was ostentatiously looking the other way and polishing glasses.

Buchanan walked to the end of the great, dark, wood bar, the soft clink of his spurs the only sound in the place. Shue, following his eyes, walked beside him. Buchanan could tell Shue and the other customers knew each other.

None of the men looked surprised. The loafer from down the street had gotten here first with the warning that Shue and a stranger were coming.

"Pardon me, sir," Buchanan told the bartender.

44

"Mr. Shue and I are looking for Mr. Pilgrim."

The bartender's bulbous eyes swiveled toward Shue, then returned. "Are you expected, mister?"

"I don't know, sir. Name of Buchanan. I'm looking for information about Joe Ford."

"Friend of Ford's?"

"Acquaintance."

The bartender glanced at one of the customers. "Jake, how about telling Mr. Pilgrim there's a gent here to see him."

A beefy youth of about eighteen detached himself from his pals and walked loosely across the room to stairs that went up. He climbed them.

"Never know if Mr. Pilgrim is busy, my man," the bartender said easily. "Like to wet your whistle?"

"Later, maybe." Buchanan put a hand lightly on Shue's shoulder, trying to look friendly. "George?"

Shue started violently, color draining from his sweaty face. "No!"

Buchanan took out a silver piece and smiled at the others. "I'd be honored to stand a round, gents."

The remaining three men looked like hard cases, heavily armed and wearing boots and pants that had never seen a day's work with cattle or horses. But his offer took them a little off guard and he could see signs of slight relaxation: a man who so easily offered drinks couldn't be a threat. They nodded and sidled back to the bar.

"You staying around, friend?" one of them, thickly bearded, asked.

"Just a short visit, I figure," Buchanan said in the same easy tone.

The bartender served beers and Buchanan paid. The man who had gone upstairs came back. He

45

eyed Buchanan. "Mr. Pilgrim will talk to you. First door, head of the stairs."

Buchanan nodded. "Come on, George," he said gently.

Shue's eyes snapped. "No."

"I think Mr. Pilgrim will want to see both of us," Buchanan told him.

Shue hesitated, fighting rage and uncertainty. Buchanan was not about to leave him here alone just yet. Shue seemed to sense that he could go quietly or be forced to go—and prove who was in charge.

Face flaming, he preceded Buchanan to the stairs.

They climbed the stairs and entered Pilgrim's office together.

It was bigger than Buchanan expected, with windows looking out over the back roof toward the mountain cliff behind it. There were some books in a rack, a huge rolltop desk and swivel chair, a big area map on one wall, a gun cabinet that looked well-stocked, a safe.

A giant of a man stood with his back to the room, looking out at the mountain. He wore a gunmetal gray suit and was billiard-ball bald. He turned as Buchanan and Shue entered. Light glittered off a big sapphire stickpin. The multiple rings on his thick fingers shone with the dull opulence of gold.

Lucas Pilgrim stood over six feet four, weighed over three hundred pounds, and had eyes as blue as his sapphire stickpin. Despite his great size he did not look fat. His face was as granitic as the mountain beyond his window.

"Mr. Buchanan, is it?" he rumbled.

Shue burst out, "He was breaking into the Ford

place! I caught him, but he tricked me! It wasn't my fault—"

"Shut up, George," Pilgrim said, his eyes never leaving Buchanan's.

"But he—"

"Shut *up, George.*"

"But—"

Pilgrim's eyes swiveled like ball bearings. "George. There is a chair outside the door. Go outside. Close the door. Sit on that chair. Wait until I call you. Don't do anything in the meantime. *Do exactly as I have told you,* and nothing more. Do you understand?"

Shue stared, rage and something else—fear—battling behind his crazed eyes.

Monolithic, Pilgrim stared, waiting.

Shue turned and went out, closing the door quietly behind him.

Pilgrim gestured Buchanan to a chair beside the rolltop. The swivel chair groaned under Pilgrim's weight as he sat down. "You obviously got the upper hand with George. Not many men do that."

"Luck."

"Yet you brought him back with you. Why?"

"I couldn't leave him there. He would have followed, bushwhacked me."

"Why didn't you kill him?"

"I didn't have to."

The ball bearing eyes were intent. "Do you kill if you must?"

"Any man will kill if he's forced to it. I haven't been forced to it."

"Today, you mean—or ever?"

Buchanan was losing patience. "I'm here because I was asked by his kinfolks in Colorado to find out what happened to Joe Ford. They told

47

me in Missoula that you would know, if anyone does. So I would have looked you up anyhow. On the way I happened on the cabin, and was looking around when Shue got the drop on me. So I brought him with me and here we are."

"You're interested in Joe Ford, you say?"

"I'm told he's dead."

"Yes. Last winter, early. Sad."

"What happened?"

"No one is quite sure. He must have fallen from high rocks. He lay out for two or three days before his wife, poor thing, finally found him. Of course by then he was quite beyond help. Two of my men located the body, gave it a proper burial, and notified the legal authorities in Missoula."

Buchanan felt a pulse. "And his wife?"

"I don't know. She was transported back to Missoula. I saw to it that there was sufficient money for a train ticket. She went away. I assume she returned home."

"She never got there."

"How very strange." Pilgrim opened a tin and offered it. "Cigar?"

Buchanan accepted and they lit up in silence. The good tobacco smoke swirled around the big room. Pilgrim, he thought, was lying to him.

"Why was your man watching the cabin?" he asked.

"The claim will expire in June. I plan to file claim to that property and two that are adjacent to it as soon as it's legally possible. In the meantime, I don't want anyone squatting."

This was interesting. "The land is valuable, then?"

"God, no. Not to anyone but a cattleman. I plan to extend my range with those acquisitions, and let some of my men build out there to make the claims meet government requirements."

Buchanan took off his hat and scratched his head. He felt deep disappointment and sadness. There was no reason for Pilgrim or anyone else to lie about Joe Ford's death. And he had seen for himself that Margaret was no longer at the cabin. But Pilgrim was not telling all of it.

"I'd like to visit the cabin once more," he told Pilgrim. "See if there are any personal effects I ought to take back to his family."

The big man nodded. "I'll have my boys help you in any way I can."

Buchanan stood. "There's the matter of Shue. I think he's going to want to get even with me."

Pilgrim nodded and raised his voice. "George?"

The door opened and Shue scurried in, looking worried.

"Mr. Buchanan is a friend of ours," Pilgrim told him. "He'll be returning to the cabin tomorrow. You and Slater will help him. You are to cooperate with him in every way. There is to be no trouble. Do you understand, George?"

Shue looked disappointed. His bright, narrow-set eyes darted to Buchanan for an instant. But his fear of Pilgrim was stronger than whatever lust he had for revenge. "Yessir," he grunted.

"That's all, George."

Pilgrim took Buchanan's hand in a bone-crunching grip. "I'm sorry you came so far for bad news, Mr. Buchanan."

"Thanks."

"As a friendly gesture, let us furnish you with a complimentary room at the Men's Best. It's the building just next door, here. You can get a good meal there and a decent room."

Buchanan's forehead wrinkled in what Pilgrim had already noted as a sign of puzzled suspicion. "Very kind of you."

Pilgrim put a hand on his shoulder as he led him to the door. "It's a cruel country sometimes. I share your grief about your dead friend and his widow . . . whatever may have happened to her. Just tell Higgins, on the desk, that I sent you. You'll be well taken care of. Then in the morning my men will call for you and help you with your sad task at the cabin."

Buchanan still looked puzzled as he left the office and went down the open steps to the saloon below.

Pilgrim stood at the railing and watched him until he was out the front door.

Then Pilgrim went downstairs and signalled to one of his men loitering at the bar. "Bert. Over here." He walked to the front of the saloon, out of earshot of the others, and Bert Atkinson followed him.

Putting his arm around the dark, lank gunman's shoulders, Pilgrim kept his voice low. "I'm going home now. Watch this Buchanan fellow. Under *no* circumstances is he to get anywhere near the Betsy Ross Cafe. You understand me?"

Atkinson, his eyes bleak, nodded. "You figure he's trouble?"

"No, no, I think everything is just fine. Just plant yourself outside his door, out of sight. Keep him away from the Betsy Ross, whatever it takes, and by tomorrow this time we'll have him on his way, and no wiser."

"Whatever it takes," Atkinson repeated stolidly.

"No violence unless there's positively no other choice. You understand me?"

"I got it," Atkinson said.

Leaning against the wall directly outside the saloon doors, where he had stopped to relight his cigar and eavesdrop, Buchanan got it too.

Tingling with discovery, he stood motionless and silent. He could hardly believe his good luck. He had known something rang false in Pilgrim's story, and had hung back in hopes of obtaining a clue. He hadn't counted on such a hell of a good tip.

Even if he had no idea what it meant.

Footfalls scraped inside the saloon. Somebody was coming toward the doors. His cigar still unlit, Buchanan hurried along the outside wall to enter the boardinghouse next door.

He made it unobserved.

Boarding his horse could wait a few minutes, he thought, approaching the counter. First he would register, just as Pilgrim had suggested. He would be a good boy and do just as he had been told.

Until it got good and dark.

51

SIX

By about nine o'clock that night, Pilgrim's only street was black as hell.

Standing unseen in his boardinghouse room window on the second floor, facing the street, Buchanan had gotten the lay of the land before darkness came.

The Betsy Ross was a one-story log building on the far side of the street just beyond the wapper jawed bridge over the creek. Walking back from the wagon yard where he had boarded his horse for the night, Buchanan had gotten a quick outside look at the place Pilgrim had said he must not be allowed to visit.

The Betsy Ross appeared from the outside to be a clean and busy cafe, nothing more and this had added to Buchanan's puzzlement. One of Pilgrim's men had shadowed him to the wagon yard, however, and he hadn't had a chance to investigate further then.

Now, with a vast and starry sky peering down the chasm formed by surrounding mountain cliffs, the street below Buchanan's window was vaguely lighted only here and there by lantern light shining from saloon windows. Most of the area below was as black as the inside of a man's hat. There was no regular traffic on the street below, although Buchanan knew there were plenty of people inside the saloons and at least a half-dozen men still inside the Betsy Ross.

He felt nervously uneasy about what he planned to do, wished there were a less threatening way. But he couldn't think of any. And if there were answers around here, he intended to have them.

Moving soundlessly in sock feet to the door of his room, he made sure the skeleton key was turned in the lock, securing it as much as any cheap boardinghouse room ever was secure. He had already turned the lantern on the wash table low, and now he twisted the metal wheel all the way, completely retracting the wick. The lamp guttered an instant, then went out.

Buchanan leaned on the bed with both hands, making it creak and groan enough to be heard by Pilgrim's man beyond the door. Then, carrying his boots, he crept to the open window and climbed out onto the balcony that the boardinghouse shared with the saloon next door.

The night air was already cold and he felt nakedly exposed. Standing against the wall of the building, feeling the heat it had retained from the day against his back, he watched a rider drift up the street and go out of sight. Men's voices came from the saloons. Three horses stood tied next door, but he couldn't see a man anywhere.

He sat on the flat roof long enough to pull on his boots. Then he moved silently to the ornate railing and put a leg over. Getting his boot toe in some of the bric-a-brac decorative woodwork of the pillar, he climbed down quickly, his feet making the slightest thumping sounds as he stepped onto the lower board porch.

Nobody challenged him.

Scalp prickling, he walked off the porch and up the street toward the Betsy Ross. Crossed the tumbling creek, whose roar engulfed him for a moment. Walked into the faint illumination coming from the sole window of the cafe, made sure his gun was ready in the right-hand holster, and moved onto the porch.

From the cafe interior came quiet men's voices and the clink of dinnerware and the warm aromas of coffee and steak and pie.

He pushed the door open and stepped inside.

The light from a half-dozen lanterns suspended from horizontal ceiling beams hit his eyes hard. He got the impression of more space than anticipated—depth to the room—a counter to the left with several men eating there, tables with red and white checked tablecloths to the right, men at three of them. Heads turned toward him as he closed the door behind himself.

His eyes quickly adjusted. The only person he recognized was the slender young lawman he had seen earlier on the street; he now stood at the end of the counter with a cup of coffee in front of him.

From a doorway behind the far end of the counter, a woman appeared carrying a tray with plates of steaming food. She was painfully thin, very pale, with great, haunted eyes and wonderful golden hair piled atop her head in a wispy knot. In the second it took her to come around the far end of the counter, tray held high, hips swaying slightly with a natural grace, Buchanan felt his insides lurch in a reaction so deep and intense that he gasped aloud.

The woman heard the sound and turned her head toward him. Their eyes met. Hers widened, hazed over with total shock and confusion, then went blank with pain.

"Margaret!"

Her lips parted. "My God—do I know you?—Yes. Are you—*Jimmy?* Is it you? Jimmy! Help me—!"

54

The tray pinwheeled in her hand and fell with a crash. Plates, food, and coffee splattered in all directions, making men scramble from the two nearest tables. Then, before anyone could react further, Margaret's eyes closed. Her body went limp from head to toe. Without a sound she collapsed in a heap on the floor.

Buchanan went a little bit crazy.

Whatever he had expected, he hadn't expected to meet the woman he had loved more than life itself. He hadn't expected to see her so thin, so pain-filled, so scared.

And he hadn't expected to see the gleam of recognition in her magnificent eyes, or to hear her cry out for help.

Men scrambled to their feet all over the cafe in response to the crash of dishes and Margaret's collapse. One of them nearest her stepped forward, reaching down toward her. He was a middle-aged man in bib overalls, with a gray beard.

Buchanan knocked another man to the floor as he crossed the space from the door to where Margaret had fallen. The farmer in overalls had almost reached Margaret with his hand. Buchanan slammed his revolver across the side of the farmer's bare head, careening him backward and into a table which overturned.

"What the hell are you doing?" somebody yelled angrily.

Falling to his knees beside Margaret, Buchanan waved his gun wildly. "Just stay the hell back, all of you!"

The farmer staggered to hands and knees. Blood streamed down the side of his face. "I was just helping her—!"

55

"And I said stay the hell *back*, everybody!"

Some of the onlookers muttered angrily. The front door slammed as somebody got out of there. Buchanan knew he was in serious trouble: Pilgrim had lied to him, had wanted him kept out of here, and now the word was spreading fast.

Maybe his life wasn't worth a sack of beans right now.

He didn't, in the instant, give a damn. Holding his Colt up menacingly he tried to examine Margaret.

Her color was like a wintry sky. He saw new lines around her eyes and mouth, the mouth he had dreamed about half his life. Her dress was made of feed sacks, high-necked, long-sleeved, with a tiny blue flower pattern in the cotton. Fine blue veins showed in her closed eyelids. One frail hand, fallen across her throat, was so thin it made Buchanan hurt.

"Margaret?" he whispered urgently, cradling her head in his arm. "I'm here. It's all right."

Somebody moved cautiously closer and squatted beside him. He swung the gun threateningly, ready to kill anybody who tried to hurt her. He looked straight into the cool gray eyes of the youthful lawman. He looked as calm as wildflowers.

"Don't try to stop me," Buchanan bit off.

"What are you going to try to do?" the younger man asked steadily.

"She's the one I came to find, my friend's wife. She doesn't belong here. I'm taking her out of here."

"Where?"

Buchanan hung up. *Where?* He had no idea.

The other man said, "My name is Holroyd. Deputy United States marshal. Nobody is going to hurt the lady."

56

"Did you hear her ask me to help her?" Buchanan demanded.

The gray eyes were unflinching. "Yes."

"I'm taking her out of here," Buchanan repeated. "I'm taking her—" *Where?*—"I'm taking her back home."

"You might be smarter to stay with her here in town until this can be sorted out."

The mention of things getting "sorted out" made Buchanan remember the man who had left the cafe, and Pilgrim's orders. He had no time to talk about alternatives. He could stay here and maybe lose Margaret again—forever—or he could do what she had pleaded—help her.

And the longer he stayed here right now, the less chance he had of getting out alive.

He decided. Scooping Margaret's fragile weight into his arms, he got to his feet. He held the revolver out in front with his right hand. "Just get the hell out of my way, Marshal."

Holroyd stood and backed aside. "Nobody is to try anything," he said quietly. "Just let this man go."

Somebody in the back of the room said, "You'll answer to Pilgrim if you let this punk take that woman outta here, Holroyd."

Holroyd's eyes flashed anger. "I'll worry about that. Nobody has to get hurt. Let him go, and don't try anything."

Margaret's unconscious form was feather-light in Buchanan's arms. He was still in shock, but determined to move. He carried her to the door, backing all the way, and stepped outside.

It was pitch dark after the bright lights in the cafe. He almost panicked because of his momentary blindness.

Margaret moaned.

57

"It's all right, it's all right," he muttered. "I've got you. Nobody is going to hurt you or hide you any more."

His eyes began to adjust. He stepped off the porch and walked awkwardly, carrying the unconscious woman across the little bridge and up the middle of the street in the direction of the wagon yard.

Bert Atkinson's chair legs hit the hall floor with a crash. "He *what?*"

"Ha's at the cafe right now!" Shorty Washburn repeated. "He walked in bigger'n Missoula and seen her right off, and she fainted—"

"Damnation!" Atkinson fled down the stairs, thinking that there would be hell to pay when Lucas Pilgrim found out he had messed up the assignment.

His only hope was to stop things before they got any worse. He reached the lower landing and started across the little lobby.

Another of Pilgrim's men, Davis Enderly, bolted in, eyes wild. "He carried her out! He's taking her out of town!"

"Shit!" Atkinson rushed onto the porch.

In the faintness of starlight, about a dozen men had spilled out of the Betsy Ross and the saloon next door. They stood in doorways, watching the street.

Buchanan had already passed Atkinson's position, and was almost to the wagon yard a block to the right.

Seething, Atkinson stepped off the porch.

A hand grasped his shoulder, stopping his next step.

He whirled to face the deputy, Holroyd. "Stay out of this, Holroyd! I've got to—"

"No," Holroyd said. "You don't have to do anything."

"Are you crazy? That woman is under Lucas Pilgrim's personal protection! If I let some crazy man carry her out of town, Pilgrim will have my ass!"

"If you try to stop that man right now, Bert, he'll shoot."

"Then—!"

"Then you'll shoot back? Right. And you'll probably win. But you're a poker player: you tell me the odds that the woman won't get hit in the gunplay."

Atkinson saw the logic, but he was beside himself. "I can't just let him leave!"

"She asked him to help her. He's taking her back to the cabin she had. You know where that is. Let him go. This can be sorted out in the morning."

Atkinson bit his tongue to stifle an obscene retort. Holroyd was right, he thought. He was helpless. But Lucas Pilgrim would go up like ten tons of gunpowder when he heard about this. Things wouldn't get "sorted out" tomorrow. They would get nasty.

The stranger named Buchanan was as good as dead right now.

In the livery barn, the scared hosteler finished saddling the nervous chestnut and whipped the cinch strap tight. Standing there in his long flannel nightshirt, he looked at Buchanan with wide, bulging eyes.

"Now what?" he asked hoarsely.

Buchanan moved close to him and held Margaret's unconscious form out to him. "You hold her. When I'm up, you hand her to me."

"This is crazy! You're crazy! You can't just kidnap somebody like this!"

59

Buchanan gently handed Margaret over. Then he swung up into the saddle. He leaned to the side and the hosteler managed to hand her up to him.

Settling her weight across the front of the saddle and his thighs, Buchanan holstered his Colt and grasped the reins. He had a moment's idea of how insane this gamble was, how easily he could be picked off once he left the barn. He didn't even know what he would do next, once he had reached the cabin . . . if he got that far.

But he had her in his arms. She had pleaded for help. There was no turning back. He would help her or die.

He touched his heels to the horse's flanks. The startled animal jolted into rough action, bursting through the front doors at a frightened canter. Buchanan turned him sharply toward the end of the street, toward the black country outside of town.

There were no shots. Buchanan needed all his horsemanship to hang on, control the animal, and keep Margaret firmly in his grasp.

They're right, he thought. *You're acting like a crazy man.*

No matter. He rode.

SEVEN

Pat Holroyd thought there would be trouble when Lucas Pilgrim heard what had happened, and he was soon proven right.

Less than an hour after Buchanan rode out of town with the woman, Holroyd, standing in his room on the second floor of the Shady Rest, saw lights high on the mountainside. He knew Pilgrim's ranch was in the valley on the far side of the mountain. The lights—torches or lanterns carried by men on horseback—marked riders coming from the Pilgrim place.

Holroyd stood in his window and watched the lights mark a curving descent through switchbacks on the wooded slopes. Within another forty minutes, the lights vanished for a while as the riders carrying them followed the river out of view from his vantage point. Then the lights appeared again, hissing pitch torches carried by horsemen entering town from the east.

Holroyd counted nine horsemen. Each carried a torch. In the steamlike clouds of crimson smoke trailing from the torches, he made out a surrey following closely. Pilgrim's.

The procession moved down the main street and stopped in front of the nearby saloon where Pilgrim headquartered. Men swung from their saddles and stood vigilant while Pilgrim clambered heavily down from the surrey and strode into the saloon and out of Holroyd's sight.

Holroyd waited, and he was not disappointed.

Somebody rapped insistently on his door. He opened it. Standing there was Henry Slater, one of Pilgrim's right-hand men. The light of Slater's lantern slanted across his face, lighting the gruesome pink socket in his left cheek where an eye was missing.

"Mister Pilgrim wants a palaver," Slater told Holroyd. His voice had no emotion of any kind in it. "You'll come now?"

Holroyd nodded. It wasn't really a question anyway.

They went downstairs, Slater trailing, and walked the few steps to the saloon. Lights blazed inside but there was no one there aside from Pilgrim's men. Holroyd counted eleven of them, which, added to the six still outside with the horses, accounted for just about all of Pilgrim's hands. They were all armed to the teeth, and he noticed other rifles and shotguns laid across some of the tables.

Upstairs, Slater rapped on Pilgrim's office door.

"Come," a voice called.

Slater opened the door, motioned Holroyd inside, and stepped back with no intention of going in with him.

Now, Holroyd thought, *come the threats and the ass-chewing.* He went in.

Lucas Pilgrim, wearing dark riding clothing that made him seem larger and more menacing than his usual business suits, sat at his rolltop desk. When he looked up to glare at Holroyd, he got to his feet. His eyes were red-rimmed, and smoky hell flickered inside them.

"That man kidnapped a woman I was trying to protect," he said.

62

"No," Holroyd countered. "She asked him to help her and he did."

"You Goddamned fool! That woman is sick in the head! She doesn't know what she wants, and now you've helped a stranger drag her off into the night to do God-knows-what to her!"

The power radiating from the much-larger man, combined with intensity of his feelings, almost rattled Holroyd's confidence. He tried to rally: "I've seen her in the cafe many times. She never seemed crazy to me. And she recognized the man. She asked him to help."

"You should have stopped him!"

"He had her in his arms. *Anyone* trying to stop him would have risked the woman's life."

Pilgrim paced to the night-black windows in the far wall, then back again. He was seething. "You'll deputize my men," he announced. "They'll rescue her and deal with Buchanan."

"No," Holroyd said immediately.

Pilgrim whirled on him with scarcely controlled rage. "Did I hear you say 'no'?"

Holroyd felt fear, but kicked it back in its hole. "I said no. You heard me right."

The baleful eyes seemed to bore through to the back of his head. "I intend to have her back. No one runs counter to my authority in this town. I own this town."

Holroyd eased in a deep breath. "I know your power here, Lucas. And I know that standing in your way isn't the healthiest thing a man can do. I could have an accident, right? Or I could ride out some morning and just disappear."

"Don't talk like a fool!" Pilgrim sneered. "I don't have people killed. I'm not a violent man. I respect law and order! I *am* law and order here!"

Holroyd stifled a grim smile. Pilgrim, he knew,

had been all for "law and order" when the vigilantes last rode; Pilgrim had given them most of their orders. A half-dozen of those lynched or shot from hiding had been men who stood between Pilgrim and ownership of some parcel of land or some monopoly in the town that bore his name.

No. What Pilgrim was really saying—and what Holroyd understood with chilling clarity—was that refusal to obey orders could easily mean the end of his appointment as a federal deputy, or the end of his life. But in either case his demise would look good, would result in no charges being filed.

It didn't feel very good, standing up to that.

Aloud, Holroyd said, "Neither of us wants trouble, then. I'll report to Marshal Turner what went on here. I'll make sure the woman isn't being mistreated. Beyond that, I just don't think I can do much for you."

"You won't deputize my men?"

"Sorry. No."

"You may be very sorry, Holroyd."

Holroyd sighed. "Maybe so."

"Reconsider. I get what I want."

"No."

"You'll never wear a badge again, and you'll never have any decent job in the Bitterroot Valley!"

"Lucas, when the day comes that I've got to kiss a man's ass to wear this badge, then that's the day I won't want it anyway." Holroyd turned toward the door.

"Where do you think you're going?"

"Right now I intend to get some sleep. In the morning I intend to check to make sure the woman is all right and still says she wants to be with Buchanan. After that, I don't know. I might be riding into Missoula to write up a report on what's happened here."

Pilgrim squared massive shoulders and seemed to gear up to make a last appeal. "There's no need for a report," he said, his lips curling in an easy grin. "All you have to do is let me handle it. No one will be hurt. I have the woman's best interests at heart."

"Probably so," Holroyd replied quietly from the door. "But somehow I think *she's* the best judge of what's good for her. And she's the one I'm going to listen to."

For a few seconds after Holroyd walked out on him, Lucas Pilgrim considered which would be the best way to kill him.

Then, with massive effort, he controlled his rage and frustration.

Be calm. Go slowly. There's too much to lose from a mistake.

Pilgrim sat at his rolltop desk and, with thick fingers that shook, unwrapped a cigar.

He was furious at Holroyd, but more angry at the stranger named Buchanan. Of course Bert should have watched him more carefully . . . but Pilgrim would deal with Bert in a moment. The question now was what to do about Buchanan.

Once that was answered, Pilgrim could have Margaret Ford back.

He never questioned that he must have her back.

He had noticed her long before Joe Ford's death, had seen her in the small Catholic church in Missoula and had been struck at once by her sun-filled hair, the way the light shone on her fair skin, how she moved with grace like no woman he had ever known, the way her dress nipped in at her tiny waist, swelled over womanly breasts. He had watched her, awestruck, throughout Mass, unable to tear his eyes away from her partially averted face,

65

her perfect profile with its sensitive chin and mouth, tiny nose, and fine forehead, the wisps of golden hair that had escaped her bonnet. Then, after Mass, he had stepped outside ahead of her and her husband and had watched her body move as she walked to the wagon, swung with lithe, animal grace up to the seat.

Lucas Pilgrim had been alone and without a woman—if you discounted the occasional and unsatisfying whore in Missoula—for more than ten years. He had thought no one would ever interest him again and that he would never risk the pain of loss again after Stella's agonized death. But all those ideas had vanished within the first minutes of seeing Margaret Ford. She stirred feelings in him that scared him with their intensity.

Joe Ford's death had been unfortunate but necessary. Pilgrim had gotten most of what he wanted out of that. Finding Margaret in such a weakened condition, needing his help, had been an unexpected bonus. Since that time he had been going very, very slowly, not only because it was good business, but for her sake.

He had been sure until tonight that patience was the key, that one day she would repay his kindness with her love. And when that day came, he had dreamed, he would have everything: the wealth, the land, the woman.

Nothing else mattered but having these things.

But Buchanan's intervention had thrown *all* of that into doubt.

Margaret had to be gotten back, Pilgrim thought. But simply rushing out and seizing her by force was out of the question for several reasons, including how it would look to the public, how it could ruin his chances of ever having Margaret's love, how it could even make certain people suspicious of his land dealings. They might then guess the truth and ruin everything.

No, he had to be clever. If violence could be avoided, he had to avoid it. Perhaps there was a way to fool Buchanan, or persuade him to leave, or buy him off. A way had to be found. Buchanan had to be gotten rid of, one way or another.

Holroyd was a problem, too. How to get rid of him. . . .

Somebody knocked on the door, dragging Pilgrim out of his reverie.

"Come," he called.

The door opened and Bert Atkinson came in slowly, hat in his hands. His spurs chinked softly on the wood floor as he came toward the desk. "Boss, I thought he was asleep."

"I told you to watch him," Pilgrim said, opening his desk drawer and taking out another cigar. He fought to keep the rage out of his voice.

"I had my chair against the wall right outside his room. He locked the door, turned out the lantern— I watched for that under the bottom of the door— and I even heard the bed squeaking. How was *I* to know he'd climb out the window and go over there?"

"It was your job to know, Bert. I gave you your instructions."

"How could I *know?*" Atkinson repeated miserably, his hat moving around a circle in his hands.

"It was your job to know."

Atkinson licked his lips. "I can fix it. I can go out there, find 'em, bring the lady back."

"And kill Buchanan?"

"Sure. Yeah. If I need to, right. Is that what you want me to do? I can do that. I'll go right now."

"No, you fool. We can't do that." Pilgrim looked into his desk drawer at the Colt he had almost

67

brought out. Now a safer method occurred to him. He closed the drawer and studied his man.

"What *do* you want me to do?" Atkinson asked miserably.

"Ride to the ranch," Pilgrim said. "Wait for me there. I'll be along shortly. We'll make plans."

Atkinson nodded eagerly. "I'll go right now."

"I'm sending Shue and Enderly with you. Are they outside?"

"Yessir, they're right downstairs."

"Good. Send them up. I want to make sure they understand that nobody is to do anything until we've planned it out. Wait for them downstairs."

"Yessir. Yessir." The relieved Atkinson hurried out.

Pilgrim waited. He discarded his earlier cigar, which in his anger he had bitten through. He had the new one going when the dwarf-like Shue and Enderly, a stoop-shouldered lout four times his size, entered the room.

"Close the door," Pilgrim ordered. "Now come close to the desk."

The twisted little man and his gorilla-like companion mutely obeyed. Pilgrim's rages were legendary, and both of them, although killers, clearly showed their fear in their sweaty pallor and wide eyes.

"You two," Pilgrim told them softly, "are riding to the ranch with Bert. The two of you will reach the ranch. Bert will never get there. On the way, he will vanish." Pilgrim eyed his two men. "Do you understand me?"

Enderly's cold eyes blinked as he absorbed the meaning. Shue's eyes changed, taking on a crafty glow, and his lips curled back from nicotine-yellowed teeth.

"He vanishes . . . permanent?" Shue said.

68

"Yes, George," Pilgrim said softly. "He is never seen or heard from again. Things like that can happen on a remote mountain road, at night, don't you agree?"

"Yeah," Shue said, his grin widening with sheer delight. "Right. It's as good as done, boss."

"Go," Pilgrim said.

The import of what had been said seemed to please Enderly, who had never gotten along with Bert Atkinson. Loosening his revolver in his holster, he lumbered toward the office door, Shue right behind him.

Pilgrim put his feet on the edge of the rolltop and puffed the cigar. In a few minutes he heard the horses' hoofs out on the road as the three men left. He returned his thoughts to how he was going to deal with Holroyd . . . and Buchanan.

He was still sitting there almost an hour later when the faintest sounds of a distant rock fall—or perhaps gunfire—two quick reports that could have been stone bouncing on stone, or shots, echoed down the canyon from far away, high up. The sounds were garbled and multiplied by echoes.

Rockslides and the sharp crack of single stones falling and smashing themselves to bits were not uncommon. Whatever Pilgrim's other men might have thought below—or whatever anyone else in town might have speculated if they had been awake to hear anything at all—was impossible to guess. Pilgrim heard no conversation about it, no called questions, no reaction of any kind.

They should have been smarter, Pilgrim thought, and gotten farther up over the pass before taking action. But the vast night silence proved that they had done the job efficiently, and no one would ever be the wiser.

His cigar was long since finished. He was tired to the bone. His plans had been made. He limped out of the office.

EIGHT

Biting his tongue with his effort to be silent, Buchanan raised the bar on the inside of the cabin door and swung the door open. He stepped outside onto the plank stoop, letting the fine drizzle coldly pepper his face.

Gray dawn hung behind the cliffs on two sides of the property. Across the stump-studded open ground that sloped down to trees beyond, through the drizzle, he could just make out a pair of does grazing the spring vegetation. He couldn't see any other signs of life. The air had a chill to it, a heaviness that matched his worry.

Turning his back to the drizzle, he rolled and lit a cigarette and inhaled it deeply.

He was in the damndest mess of his life, and knew it.

He hadn't thought when he walked into the cafe and got the incredible shock of seeing Margaret. Her pallor, her thinness, and her cry for help had triggered instinctive reactions. He knew he should have looked ahead. But how did you look ahead when you were crazy with surprise and fear for somebody you loved so much?

Puffing on his smoke, he reviewed things.

He wouldn't have gotten out alive, he thought, if that young deputy marshal had not been on the scene. Why had he helped? Buchanan had no idea. But he could imagine how much trouble the man was in today.

Buchanan had ridden out of Pilgrim and headed straight for the cabin. Carrying Margaret farther was out of the question. All he had thought of at the moment was getting her away from Pilgrim and into a warm place. So he had made it to the cabin, pried the front door off again, carried her inside, and found a lantern that still had some oil in it. In the feeble yellow light he'd put dry wood in the fireplace and got it going while Margaret lay unconscious on the dusty, rodent-chewed bed.

She had stirred, then, awakened, and the scope of his predicament had broadened.

Buchanan mentally reviewed it. But he didn't get far before a small, sharp cry of alarm sounded inside the cabin at his back.

"Joe?" Margaret's voice called shrilly. "Where are you? What am I—oh, God!"

Buchanan flipped his cigarette into the rain and hurried back inside.

Margaret, still wearing her cafe dress, now rumpled, with hair awry and eyes puffy and disoriented, stood in the middle of the floor. She stared at him with eyes that held no recognition.

"Joe?" she cried shrilly. "Where is Joe?"

It was like a reenactment of last night.

Buchanan went to her and took her in his arms, hugging her tight, trying to drive the demons out with his own strength. "It's all right, babe. It's all right. You're safe, Peggy."

The old childhood name seemed to lance through her confusion. She drew back from him, wild eyes staring into his face. "Who—*Jimmy?*"

"You're safe," Buchanan repeated gently, half supporting her frail weight.

With a sob she let him walk her back to the bed. She sat on its edge, holding her face in her hands. "God—I woke up and I was back here and I didn't remember—I couldn't figure out where I was or what had happened—"

"Do you remember now?" Buchanan asked, sitting beside her and taking her icy hands in his own.

She stared at him again, her eyes filled with sorrow. "Yes."

"I found you in that cafe, and—"

"He didn't come home," she said with the flatness of a metronome. "I waited. He didn't come home. He had been late before. I waited all day. In the night I was alone. He didn't come home. I had to do something. I started out to look for him. I looked all day."

"All right, all right," Buchanan said, trying to calm her frantic, onrushing voice.

"I didn't find him," she went on as if driven. "Not that day. The next. I found him the next. He was by the creek. High up. There had been an animal—a bear, a wolf, I don't know what—and the animal had *chewed* on him. It had—his arm—it had *eaten* his arm off, and there was blood, and the sun had been shining on him, and he was dead, and I was alone, and I didn't know what to do—"

"I know," Buchanan crooned. "I know." Inside he was recoiling from the vision of what she must have found, the depth of her horror and shock. *No wonder she's half-crazy.* "You don't have to talk about it."

Margaret studied his face, and her expression became one of quiet wonderment. "You found me. I was in the cafe. You found me. You've brought me home."

"You need rest," Buchanan told her. "Later I'm going to take you into Missoula. We'll find some-

73

body to look after you. I'll find out how Joe fell, and what the deal is on this land."

"The map," she said. She looked around, frantic. "I hid the map. Where did I hide the map?"

"What?"

"The map! The map! Where did I hide the map?"

"Peggy, babe," Buchanan groaned, "I don't know what you're talking about."

"We had a fight," Margaret said.

"What?"

"We had a fight. Remember? You said you wanted to marry me, but you wanted to save money first. I was hurt. Joe wanted to marry me right away. Then I heard you had gone to the dance with Patsy Eberhart. I came to the farm. You said you hadn't. I said you had only strung me along—"

Buchanan stared in dismay as she rattled on, repeating verbatim things that had been done and said more than three years ago. It was like her mind had no tracks, and ran randomly in whatever direction her momentum took it.

". . . and then we came here to Montana," she finished. She studied his face. Tears sprang from her eyes. "If I could just remember where I hid the map! Why can't I remember?"

"I want you to sit right here and rest easy," Buchanan told her. "There's some canned stuff on the shelves; that ought to still be good. I'll rustle us up some kind of breakfast."

"Yes," she said in a voice that was almost inaudible, and eerily calm. "I think I should eat."

He got up and explored the shelving and cabinets. In the jars were potatoes, what looked like squash, jelly, maybe canned fish. He got the fire going smartly again, went outside and dipped fresh water out of the barrel that drained the roof, then came back inside and set it to boil. He opened the jar of preserved fish and put the contents in a skillet and started them frying, figuring they would provide enough fat to prepare the potatoes. He wished fervently for coffee.

"There have been mice," Margaret said calmly. "No other critters burrowing in, though."

"I'll have to clean, if we're going to live here. Are we going to live here, Jimmy?"

He turned to look at her. She smiled. She was in another compartment of her damaged mind, and her question cut to the middle of his heart. For a crazy instant he thought he could do just that—live with her here, hunt and farm a little, and not let anybody else get near her. And if she was mad, so what? When she was partly lucid she would be like this, so soft, tender, trusting, beautiful. And he would be good to her, hold her in the night, nurse her back to health, have her forever.

"Are we?" she repeated in the same childlike tone, smiling.

He shook himself mentally. Sudden dreams like that were crazy, as crazy as she was. Now she had him raving too.

What kind of a man, he asked himself, would want a mad woman? What kind of man would take advantage like that? He loved her so much, he was thinking like a maniac.

His agenda had to be quite different. Dumping the hot fish out onto a platter so he could start the potatoes, he reviewed it.

First, he had to find a safe place for her, a place where she could have rest and care and protection from Pilgrim.

Second, he had to find out how Joe had died.

Third, he had to learn if this cabin and this land were still Margaret's property, and, if so, what she wanted to do about them. Pilgrim would buy them,

75

it had sounded like. Would she want to sell?

And that raised all the other questions.

Why was Pilgrim interested in this land, if it was as useless as it looked?

Why had Pilgrim kept Margaret working in his town, hidden from strangers? Did that have to do with the land . . . or with some darker scheme he had had in mind for her?

Could Margaret's mind be restored?

How was Pilgrim going to react to the night's events? Was Buchanan's life worth a plugged nickel this morning?

How was he going to get her safely to town? How was he going to find someone to care for her—someone trustworthy? How was he going to learn the truth about Joe? How was he going to keep Margaret safe? How was he going to get her sane and free of this place and back home, if that was where sanity told her she wanted to be?

How was he going to stay alive long enough to do any of it?

He turned and looked at her, sitting there on the bed.

She smiled, and it was like gentle spring sunlight. "I'm glad you came, Jimmy. Lucas was good to me. He means no harm. He wants to buy the land. But I know about the map. I don't trust him."

"What map is that, Peggy?" Buchanan asked. "You've already mentioned it three or four times."

"It's the map I hid, and can't remember where I hid it," she told him calmly. "You know. The one I found when I found Joe, where Joe had been murdered."

"Murdered?" Buchanan repeated sharply. "I heard he fell."

"No." She looked into some private hell and shuddered. But then she came right back. "He was

76

murdered—shot. He had been shot in the face."

It rocked Buchanan. The mental picture of her discovery in the mountains took on new clarity and horror. *You knew, Buchanan. It never rang true, that stuff about an accidental fall.*

But now that he knew this part of the truth, what did it mean?

Before he could say anything, there was the sound of hoofbeats outside, a horse walking up near the front of the cabin.

Margaret heard them at the same instant.

And screamed.

Buchanan moved past her, snaking out his revolver, and opened the front door a crack. It was Holroyd, the deputy marshal who had prevented bloodshed last night. The cold drizzle made his big red roan steam as he reined up.

"It's all right," Buchanan told Margaret. "It's a friend."

She stood with her hand to her mouth. "It's . . . not . . . ?"

"No. It's a friend. Believe me."

She gulped air and relaxed, her fear abated.

Buchanan swung the door wide. "Holroyd. You're alone?"

The deputy nodded and swung out of the saddle. "I think I'm more alone than I've ever been in my life, friend."

"What brings you here?"

"Nobody sent me, if that's what you're thinking."

"What, then?"

"We need to palaver. I don't want you dead. Or her dead. Or me, either."

That made sense. Buchanan stepped out of the doorway and holstered his gun. "Tie to the post, there, and come on in. I'm making some breakfast."

Holroyd, hat in hand, came cautiously into the cabin. He studied Margaret with keen intensity. She returned his look with haunted uncertainty.

"We've met," she said finally.

"In the cafe," Holroyd told her. "You served me several times."

Buchanan pulled the skillet off the fire. The potatoes were seared and steaming. "Breakfast."

Margaret went to the table and sat on a packing-box chair. Buchanan dished up the canned food. He told Holroyd, "There's plenty."

Holroyd shook his head and focused on Margaret. "Mrs. Ford—you are Mrs. Ford, right?"

"Yes."

"Last night you asked this feller to help you. He's brought you here. I need to make sure that's what you want, that you aren't being held against your will."

"No," Margaret said quickly. "I want—this. Jim is my friend. He's helping me."

"I never got the idea you were being held in Pilgrim against your will."

Margaret's big eyes registered surprise. "No! I wasn't! I—after my husband died, I didn't have anyone. Mr. Pilgrim came. He offered to get me a job in the town. I'm . . . not quite well. I wanted to save my money, earn a way home. I wanted to go home to Colorado. I wanted to stay here in the valley. I wanted the job. I didn't want the job. I was going to save my money but I didn't have any money left after I paid my rent and food. I—" She stopped and waved a thin hand over her eyes as if trying to brush away cobwebs. "I don't think I'm making a lot of sense."

78

Holroyd shot Buchanan a questioning glance.

"She'll get better," Buchanan told him. "I'm taking care of her now."

The deputy turned back to Margaret. "You want to stay with this man?"

"I — yes."

"You're not being held against your will."

"No!"

Holroyd nodded. "That's what I had to be sure of."

"What happens now?" Buchanan demanded. "With Pilgrim, I mean."

"He isn't happy."

"Is he coming after me? After her?"

"Not directly, I think. Lucas Pilgrim is smarter than that."

Buchanan spooned hot food onto another tin plate for himself.

"What are your plans?" Holroyd asked.

"Is there a place in Missoula where she would be safe, get good care?"

"The nuns have a new place. Hospital and chapel. St. Patrick. Used to be the courthouse. Then it was a chicken coop. They've cleaned it up pretty good. They've got a few patients. Couple of old folks, a crazy man."

Buchanan started eating, standing by the fire. "They have a doctor?"

"Not their own. Of course there's one in town. He goes there."

"What do they charge?" Buchanan was thinking of his skinny purse, and the need he now had to buy a horse and saddle. "Are they high?"

"They're free."

"Free?"

"Donations. They go around the mines, get donations."

79

Buchanan watched Margaret put a dainty fork of food between her lips. He was intensely aware of her dependency. "Might be the place."

Holroyd nodded. "They can help her . . . if anybody can."

"What about you?"

Holroyd blinked. "What about me?"

"Are you in big trouble for helping us last night?"

A grim smile transformed the youthful deputy's lean face. "I'm alive so far, I don't think Pilgrim wants trouble with the federal law. He don't control that like he does the sheriff's office."

Buchanan forked in more food. It wasn't very good, but it was going to be a long day. "Thanks for the warning."

Holroyd put on his hat. "I'll be going. Just wanted to make sure I had the lay of the land right."

Buchanan went outside with him. The drizzle was almost stopped, and high sunlight tried to poke through the low clouds.

"You ought to be able to make it to town without her getting too wet," Holroyd said, untying his reins.

"Thanks again for the help."

The deputy swung into the saddle and looked down at him. "About all I can do, friend. From now on you're on your own."

Buchanan smiled. "I can take it from here."

"Mister, I wouldn't be in your boots for all the tea in China." Holroyd turned his horse and moved away, downslope.

Buchanan watched him ride out of sight. Then he turned to reenter the cabin. As he did so, something briefly glinted high in the wooded mountain to the west. Pulse racing, he looked sharply, but couldn't spot the gleam again.

He went on into the cabin. "Eat up," he said cheerfully. "Then we'll head for town."

The cheer was a good act, he hoped, because inside he wasn't feeling cheerful at all. The instant's gleam of something in the distant mountain timber had changed a lot of things, brought him back to reality.

He would have bet everything he had that the glint had been sunlight briefly reflected off the lens of a spyglass. Somebody up there was watching them.

NINE

Riding double, with Margaret clinging behind him in the saddle, Buchanan let the rent horse pick a slow and easy gait that would spare him a beating on the ride back to Missoula. It was late in the afternoon when they arrived. Margaret was ashen with fatigue.

Buchanan found the white frame building that now served as St. Patrick Hospital. A black-clad nun of about fifty met him and Margaret in the small front office.

"You work alone here, Sister?"

Her smile was wan but genuine. "There are four of us presently. We are Sisters of Providence. Part of our support comes from St. Ignatius, and the local people have been good. With God's help, we are far from alone."

She showed them around. The hospital had virtually no equipment beyond beds and the most primitive medicines. But the building was stout and clean. Margaret examined everything with the unworldly calm that sometimes descended over her, as if she were only half in this universe.

"If we could talk alone, Sister?" Buchanan said softly, after the brief tour.

The nun nodded in understanding. "Of course." She hailed a younger nun across the ward. "Sister Grace! If you could take Mrs. Ford into the next

82

room and begin getting her information?"

Once they were alone, Buchanan tried to explain about Margaret's mental condition. The nun, Sister Immaculata, interrupted gently. "Peace, rest, good care and prayer, Mr. Buchanan. They work wonders. She will be very well cared for. And loved. Then, with God's grace—"

"There is another problem, sister. An important man locally, Lucas Pilgrim—"

"Oh, of course. Mr. Pilgrim has been most generous to our cause."

Buchanan gritted his teeth. "Mr. Pilgrim wishes Mrs. Ford to be in his care. Mrs. Ford has chosen to be with me. Mr. Pilgrim might come here and ask you to release her into his custody. Is there any chance you would do that against Mrs. Ford's wishes?"

Flint appeared in the older nun's eyes. "You have entrusted this woman to us, Mr. Buchanan. She is clearly not your prisoner. We will keep your trust."

"Sister, I couldn't ask for more." Buchanan put a twenty dollar gold piece on the desk.

"Payment is not necessary."

Buchanan grinned at her. It was a hell of a lot of money. He considered it a good investment.

A few minutes later he walked out into the chill Montana twilight and untied the worn-out chestnut. He led the animal up the street toward the livery barn four blocks away.

He was shaken by the farewell with Margaret. He had explained earlier that she would be safest with the nuns, and would get treatment. And she agreed with all that. But when he hugged her to say goodbye, her brave front cracked and she began crying silently, shaking against him.

"You're going to get well," he told her. "You're safe."

"I know. I know. I'm just scared."

"You need rest. Medicine. I'll be close by."

She stared at him with eyes that suddenly had the frightening dazed quality. "Is it Christmas?"

"What?"

"Is it Christmas? Have I forgotten Christmas?"

So she had shunted into another of her dimensions. He had walked out with a feeling of despair.

The nuns would get her better if anyone could, he thought, walking closer to the livery barn. Right now he had to concentrate on other problems.

The same runty operator was in the barn when he walked the drooping horse in and pulled the saddle.

"You didn't give him oats," the man said accusingly.

"No. Sorry."

"You kept 'im outside last night, an' you've used him hard."

"He hasn't been mistreated. He's just tired."

Muttering, the operator started to lead the chestnut away.

"I need to buy a horse," Buchanan said.

The man glared with weasel eyes. "Got none for sale."

Buchanan figured he was just angry about the chestnut. He figured there were other places to buy a mount, and he had a little bit of lingering evening light left to do it in.

Forty minutes later, after trying three other barns, he began to realize how wrong he was.

"There are horses all over the corral!" he angrily told the last hosteler.

"None for sale," the man said, eyes opaque with dishonesty.

"Goddammit, why does your sign say they're for sale, then?"

"Buddy," the man said, "I don't make the rules. I just obey 'em."

Buchanan walked out of the barn with the feeling that he had been very, very slow catching on.

Somebody had gotten to the livery operators ahead of him. *He's tall, thin, wears a Texas rig, name of Buchanan. You don't do business with him, because if you do, you get no more business of ours. Savvy?*

Night came as he walked stiffly up the main street, his anger mixed with desperation and a gnawing sense of hopelessness. Most of his gear and ruck were still in a room in Pilgrim, and he had a snowball's chance of ever seeing them again. He had his money in the belt under his underwear, his gun, a few shells. Nothing else. If Lucas Pilgrim was powerful enough to block his purchase of a horse, Pilgrim could block just about anything he wished.

What the hell chance was there against that kind of odds?

He kicked his discouragement down and walked into the boardinghouse where he had stayed his first night in Missoula. There was a different man behind the counter, and he didn't look sleepy.

Why did Buchanan get the feeling the man had been watching for him?

"I need a room for the night."

The man was powdery thin, possibly sixty, with shifty eyes that didn't meet his. "Rentin' only by the week."

"When did *that* rule go in?"

"Today." Sweat glistened on the older man's face, betraying nervousness he otherwise hid well. "New rule. Just today."

Buchanan swallowed his anger. "I'll take it for a week, then."

"Sorry. Full up."

Buchanan pointed to the boxes behind the counter. "How come there are keys in seven or eight of those boxes, then?"

"Full up! I told you, we're full—"

The clerk's words were cut off in his windpipe as Buchanan grabbed him by the throat and dragged him halfway over the counter. "Listen, you old bastard. I want a room and I want a room now."

The old man's eyes rolled in terror. "All right! All right! Put me down! Lemme down! I'll see what I can do!"

Buchanan let go, and he slithered back across the counter, just escaping a nasty fall. With fright-filled eyes he watched as Buchanan filled out the register, tossed a week's room rent on the counter, and took the key.

"It's room six—just at the top of the hall."

"Thanks for nothing." Buchanan went up the steps.

The room was no better and no worse than the other one he had had here, or in a dozen other places. A rope bed, a dresser, a rack to hang something in if a man had clothes to hang, one chair, a washbasin and pitcher, a mirror with a crack along one side.

Buchanan locked the door, shoved the chair under the knob, and poured water into the basin. It was cool and fresh and it felt good on his hot, angry face. Maybe he had been reckless, he thought, but there was just so far a man ought to be pushed.

He reached for the towel on the dresser.

Somebody knocked on the door.

"Who is it?" he called, still seething.

"Sheriff," the beefy voice answered. "Open up, now."

What the hell?
Buchanan pulled the chair out from under the doorknob, turned the key, and opened up.

He found himself staring into the twin caverns of the business end of a double-barrel shotgun. He froze.

The man behind the shotgun was his own height, but a hundred pounds heavier, with a belly hanging over his shell belt. He was older, perhaps forty, with long, shaggy gray hair that hung in an oily mass behind his Mexican-style sombrero. Wide-set, canny eyes peered out from under a shelf of bushy gray eyebrows. He had a thick beard, coarse lips. His shirt, vest, and pants were a dusty dark blue. A badge on his vest caught the light.

"You've got the wrong room," Buchanan said.

"Wrong." The lawman poked him in the midsection with the barrels of the shotgun, hard. "Back up and keep your hands high."

Still caught by surprise, Buchanan obeyed. The lawman came in with him, keeping the gun leveled on his midsection. "Now just lift that iron out of your holster and put it on the bed real slow. I'm the nervous type, son, so don't do anything that might make Betsy, here, go off."

"Who the hell are you, anyway?"

"The name's Abercrombie. Sheriff of Missoula County. And you're Buchanan, J. Get the iron on the bed, son. I'm getting twitchy."

Beginning to seethe, Buchanan obeyed carefully.

"Fine. Now hold your hands as high as you can, and turn around. With your back to me. Good." A quick hand patted Buchanan down, found his belt knife, extracted it, and tossed it onto the bed with the Colt.

"Sheriff, do you want to tell me what the hell is—"

The shotgun rammed into his back with painful force, catching his breath in his throat. "Son, you just walked into this establishment and terrorized that clerk downstairs and plumb *bullied* him into giving you this room. Now, we don't do stuff like that in Missoula no more."

"There were plenty of rooms!"

"A man's got the right to refuse service to anybody he wants."

"Why did he turn me down? Did you ask him that?"

The sheriff sounded weary. "A man owns a place, he don't need no reason. You broke the law, son, bullying him that way. You're getting outta here. Now."

Buchanan turned to confront Abercrombie. "Am I under arrest, then?"

"Management says it wants no trouble. You just git, and they'll let bygones be bygones."

Buchanan hung onto his temper. "What about my money?"

The sheriff blinked, stupid. "Money?"

"I paid for a week in advance."

"I don't know nothing about that."

"If you're throwing me out, I've got my money due back!"

"I guess maybe you should have thought of that before you created this disturbance. Any judge would say you forfeited your deposit when you created trouble. Any judge would say that."

Buchanan cracked. He took a step toward the lawman, pointing at him. "Now listen—!"

He got no farther. The lawman moved like a bull.

The twin barrels of the shotgun jammed into Buchanan's stomach below the belt. Quick agony buckled him, and Abercrombie kept coming forward, bowling him over the corner of the bed and onto the floor on his back.

The sheriff moved the muzzles hard up under Buchanan's chin and shoved hard enough to send waves of pain through him. "Son, it ain't too late to teach you respect for the law."

Buchanan froze, breathing hard. Death had never been any closer. This man might talk slowly, act dumb. But the light in his eyes was the pure malevolence of a cruel man driven by his own demons. For a moment it was touch and go. The shotgun trembled. Craziness danced in those eyes.

Then the moment passed. Abercrombie relaxed the pressure. "You're new here. Maybe you're just stupid. I'm giving you one more chance, I don't know why. I guess it's just because I'm a good person." He stepped back, the shotgun still leveled. "Git up. Pick up your stuff, there. I'll take care of the gun and knife. Walk out of here ahead of me, right down the steps, right outside."

Buchanan obeyed. The stairs creaked loudly under their steps. The tiny lobby was empty, but he felt somebody watching from the black doorway behind the desk. He had seldom been any angrier, or felt more helpless.

Outside on the porch it was now fully dark, and across the street piano music racketed from a saloon. Abercrombie put his shotgun in the crook of his arm and punched the bullets out of Buchanan's revolver, then tossed it unexpectedly at him, hitting him in the gut with it. Buchanan narrowly caught it before it slid to the ground. The sheriff flipped the knife at him, but he couldn't catch that, too. It clunked to the boards at his feet.

Buchanan holstered his empty weapon and bent to pick up the knife.

The shotgun barrels touched the back of his head as he started to raise up, and he froze again, half-bent.

"I hope you appreciate this chance, Abercrombie told him. "If you go off half-cocked again, and start any more trouble, you go in the hole. Remember that."

Biting his tongue to hold back what he wanted to say, Buchanan did not move. The pressure of the shotgun left his head. He looked up. The sheriff already turned away and was walking off the porch, his fat ass swaying with each step.

Buchanan stood very still, his breath short in his chest and his heart crashing at the speed of an express train. Everything in him wanted to hit back. But he couldn't. Not right now.

That would have been just what the sheriff wanted.

The sheriff — and the man who had given him his orders, Lucas Pilgrim.

A woman's coarse laughter echoed out of the saloon across the street, bringing Buchanan back to the present. He was still as angry and frustrated as he had ever been in his life, but he struggled to get control, to think things out.

He figured there couldn't be any doubt that he had failed to find a horse for sale and then been turned away from a room because orders had been given. And Pilgrim had to be the source.

So Pilgrim was getting even.

Or it might be more than that. What could he hope to achieve besides petty revenge?

Buchanan knew at once. Pilgrim could make life

so damned miserable for him that he would be forced out of Missoula and the valley entirely.

Leaving Margaret alone and helpless again?

Leaving her land for Pilgrim?

Buchanan limped off the porch and started up the street toward the west, thinking that there was too much he didn't know, and too many people against him. Who had killed Joe Ford? Why? What the hell had Margaret been talking about when she mentioned a lost map of some kind?

He had to ask her that, just as soon as she was well enough.

Right now, the immediate problem was finding a place to stay tonight.

Maybe, he thought, Pilgrim hadn't been able to buy off or scare every boardinghouse in town.

Thirty minutes and three more tries later, he wasn't so sure.

Oh, he had been careful to hide his anger, which was growing again, to turn away meekly, walk out without making a scene that would give Abercrombie his chance. But he was furious after leaving the third place, and was beginning to wonder if he could make it through the night under a bridge, or in an alley.

Possibly if he had not been so angry and preoccupied, he would have been more alert when he started across the dark alley intersection and they hit him.

TEN

In the office of St. Patrick Hospital, Sister Immaculata and Dr. Abraham Stone conferred over her desk. A candle guttered on a saucer nearby, providing yellow light that fluttered, sending gargoyle shadows across the ceiling and walls.

"And you say her name is Margaret Ford?" Stone asked.

Sister Immaculata inclined her head slightly. "Mrs. Joseph Ford."

"But her husband is dead?"

"So I understand. She was brought to us by a man named Buchanan . . . a friend."

Stone's thick hand formed a fist on the desktop. "He was no friend if he kept her from medical attention so long. From what she told me during her lucid period, it's been months since her husband died!"

"Yes," Sister Immaculata agreed. "But Mr. Buchanan arrived here only a day or two ago, he said. And he found Mrs. Ford only yesterday or the day before that."

"Where was she? My God—excuse me, Sister—surely she hasn't lived alone since her husband's death!"

"She was in Pilgrim."

Stone's jaw dropped. "What kind of place is *that* for a woman in her condition?"

"Mr. Pilgrim himself took interest in her," Sister Immaculata said calmly. "She was working there in a cafe of some sort that he owns."

The doctor shook his head, his expression becoming more grim. "I begin to get the picture."

"I doubt it," Sister Immaculata told him. "Mr. Pilgrim seems to have truly taken a Christian interest in her case. He gave her a job and let it be known that she was under his protection, nothing more."

"She told you this?"

"In part. Then an hour ago, Mr. Pilgrim's attorney, Mr. Laird, came to call. He explained details and made a contribution to ensure her care."

Dr. Stone leaned back with a snort.

"You doubt Mr. Pilgrim's Christian intentions, Doctor?"

"Sister, on the day Lucas Pilgrim cares about anybody but himself, you'll see elephants flying to the moon and Flatheads going to college."

Sister Immaculata gave him a thin smile. "Be that as it may. Mr. Buchanan was worried that someone, perhaps Mr. Pilgrim, might try to take Mrs. Ford out of the hospital, or perhaps even harm her. After talking with the attorney Laird, I feel reassured. Whatever Mr. Pilgrim's interests or motives may be, it seems clear to me that he is not going to interfere with her treatment here."

"You're more confident than I am," Dr. Stone said. "I don't know why a man like Pilgrim would be interested in a woman like Mrs. Ford except for the obvious, uh, well—she is an attractive woman, even in her present debilitated state. But I wouldn't trust Lucas Pilgrim farther than I could throw a goat."

"Doctor, I feel sure she will be left alone here

93

to recover." Sister Immaculata studied him. "She *will* recover?"

Stone scowled. "Physically, yes. She's very thin, frail. She's eaten too little and worked too hard, and her nervous condition has simply exhausted her. No problem there that a few days' rest, and peace and quiet, won't start to cure. Her mental condition is something else."

"I spoke with her an hour or so ago and she seemed calmer than when she arrived. And very rational."

"For the first few minutes I talked with her, Sister, I thought she was as sane as you or I. But then, like a switch had been thrown, she started to talk about things that made no sense at all. And she had partial amnesia. Things have happened to her. The death of her husband was a profound shock."

"Will her mind recover?"

Dr. Stone dodged the question. "The rest and good care will help. The mind is a marvelous, complex instrument. It has healing powers of its own. I'll see her every day. Perhaps the more she is around people like you and the other sisters, the faster her mind will mend itself."

"Will it be a long process?"

"She could recover in hours or days, as if spontaneously. I've seen that happen. On the other hand, it could take months — years — with these relapses."

"But she *will* recover fully, Doctor?" Sister Immaculata insisted.

Stone met the nun's gentle eyes. "I have no idea," he admitted.

In his business office over the legal suite belonging to Laird and Carmichael, Attorneys at Law, Lucas Pilgrim paced the gleaming hardwood floor and smoked a cigar, waiting.

Interference by an outsider like Buchanan was infuriating, Pilgrim thought. But now that his initial rage and frustration had passed, Pilgrim could begin to see that the situation might even be turned to his advantage.

He still wanted Margaret Ford. No two ways about that. Margaret touched chords inside him that he had thought were dead. Her gentleness, her sweet vulnerability, her underlying loyalty and strength — all of her best qualities moved him. She would make a fine wife for him, a woman he could be proud of, who could even give him children. And the cool beauty of her profile, along with her graceful arms and legs and the secret swell of her breasts, filled him with desire to possess her in that way, too.

If he played his cards just right, he could still have her, he thought. But first he had to deal with this fool Buchanan and make sure of the land. Only then could he afford the luxury of personal wants and desires. Too much had already been done to allow personal passion to interfere with —

His thoughts were interrupted by the harsh sound of footsteps on the back stairs. He walked quickly to the window, verified who was coming, and unlocked the door.

By the time the door opened, he had walked back to sit behind his large, flat desk on the far side of the room.

George Shue was first through the door, his shotgun in the crook of his arm, his mad eyes glinting as he grimaced jerkily, revealing jagged teeth. Shue literally hopped into the room, chuckling.

Next came Jake Murnan, beefy, sloppy, carrying another shotgun. Behind him struggled one-eyed Henry Slater and the chill Davis Enderly, and between them they supported the slumped, almost unconscious form of Jim Buchanan.

Buchanan's hat was gone and his head hung, blood dripping from his nose and mouth. Another ugly wound seeped bright red on the side of his skull. His shirt was half-torn off and his lower body, covered with mud and blood, seemed incapable of supporting his weight.

Slater and Enderly dragged him partway across the room and then simply let go. The sound of his bones hitting the floor was thick and ugly.

Pilgrim could hardly have been more pleased.

"What have you done?" he cried as if aghast. "I told you I wanted to *see* this man! What gave you the idea you were supposed to attack him?"

Buchanan heard Pilgrim's words through the pain. He managed to raise his head off the floor. He looked up and got Pilgrim partly in focus through a pink blood-haze. His chest felt on fire, worse than the time he had cracked two ribs while breaking a horse. He couldn't see quite straight. Pain filled his skull and pelvis. He had already vomited, and felt like he might again.

He hadn't had a chance. They had been all over him, and the first blow to the head with a revolver barrel had stunned him before he could make a move. After that, the beating had been systematic and brutal.

Lucas Pilgrim came around his desk and swung back into blurry focus as he knelt beside Buchanan. "Mr. Buchanan! This is terrible! Please accept my apologies, sir!"

Buchanan managed to sit up. The big man's fake concern struck him as wildly funny. *All right, just go along with the joke. No harm done. Everybody get some laughs, here.*

Through split lips he muttered, "No harm done."

Pilgrim put his hands under Buchanan's arms and lifted him up to a chair as if he weighed nothing at all. The pain was extraordinary. "Get this man a drink, quickly! Somebody wet a cloth from the basin on my desk. Just sit quietly, Mr. Buchanan, and we'll help you all we can."

Buchanan let them meddle with him. When the henchman named Enderly handed him a small glass of whisky, he drank it, shuddering. It wasn't bad whisky, but the blood in his mouth did not make a good mixer.

"Good God," Pilgrim murmured, still all phony solicitousness. "I'm afraid you've lost a couple of teeth, sir. And that eye looks bad." He poked at Buchanan's chest. "Does this hurt?"

"Yes!"

"I think we should send for Dr. Stone. Jake, go and —"

"No doctor," Buchanan managed. "I'm all right."

Pilgrim went to a humidor on the desk and brought back a cigar. "A smoke might help."

"I'll smoke my own." Buchanan fished his Bull Durham and papers out of his shirt pocket. They were soggy with either mud or blood, but as his head began to clear he was far too angry to smoke one of Pilgrim's cigars.

Pilgrim turned on his men. "Whose idea was

this? What kind of people must Mr. Buchanan think we are, to treat him this way? Goddammit, we're trying to build a fine, modern city here! Law and order are of the highest priority!"

Buchanan cracked a match and lit his smoke. "You can cut the act, Pilgrim."

"I assure, you, my friend, that despite disagreements we may have between us—"

"I said you can *cut it*." Buchanan's head suddenly was crystal clear, and his anger was a shimmering force all through him. "Tell me what you had me dragged up here for."

Pilgrim clung to his act, eyes wide with feigned worry. "I hoped to explain my position, sir, vis-à-vis the Ford land, the entire situation with reference to Widow Ford, et cetera. We have no reason to be in conflict."

"I'm real glad to hear that." The sarcasm dripped.

"When you feel better in the morning, Mr. Buchanan, perhaps we can have the discussion I had hoped we might enjoy this evening. I assure you that this was a tragic misunderstanding. If you change your mind about seeing the doctor, or if you have any other need—"

"Talk now."

"In your condition—"

"Whatever you have to say, Pilgrim, spit it out."

"Are you *sure*—"

"Talk!"

Pilgrim's massive shoulders slumped. He glanced at his men. "Outside. Wait."

Boots scraped the floor as they filed out onto the exterior stairway. The door closed behind Shue, the last one out.

Pilgrim went to his desk and sat behind it,

thick hands folded on its surface. "You're sure you feel well enough—"

"For the last time, *talk*."

The huge man sighed with bogus regret. "When Mr. Ford died accidentally, Mr. Buchanan, I heard about it right away. I have great plans for the area to the east of here. My community out there, joined with Missoula, will form a garden spot of the Northwest. One day there may be more efficient methods which will allow us to enlarge our mining operations. In the meantime, the land has great potential for large-scale cattle operations. I keep my eye on things, do what I can to help settlers, encourage orderly growth and lawful behavior."

"What's the point?" Buchanan demanded. Shock was wearing off and his pain was getting worse. "You heard Joe Ford had died, and you wanted his land. That's it, isn't it?"

"I want his land, yes. It isn't vital to me, but if it becomes available, it would cement other holdings I have in the area. But I assure you, my friend, that isn't why I helped Mrs. Ford."

"Yeah. I think I have an idea about why you helped Mrs. Ford."

Pilgrim spread his hands. "She was alone. Helpless. I gave her shelter and helped her find a position of employment."

"*Is* there a point here somewhere, Pilgrim?"

Pilgrim sighed. "Mrs. Ford is, I understand, being cared for at the hospital." He paused for a reply, but Buchanan didn't give him one. "You are her friend. So my responsibility for her well-being is at an end."

"You've got that right."

"Mr. Buchanan, I do want that land. I want to

help you help her. Therefore I asked my men to locate you and invite you here this evening to make a proposition that should help all of us."

"That being?"

"Sell me the Ford claim. It's worthless as anything but an addition to my rangelands. With the money I am prepared to offer—and it's very generous—you can take poor Mrs. Ford out of here, to some larger community with more medical facilities or home, if you feel that would be better for her." Pilgrim spread his hands again. "I would have what I want. Mrs. Ford would be safe. Your problems would be solved. What could be better?"

"There's only one problem," Buchanan told him.

"What?"

"I don't know if Margaret wants to sell to you."

"But of course she would, if she were wholly sane!"

"I find that hard to believe for sure. You had her where you wanted her for months. If you're offering such a good deal for worthless land, *why didn't she sign it over to you long ago?*"

"The woman is not well! That's why, after sober reflection, I welcome your arrival, sir. You can take the action that she would take if she were in control of all her faculties!"

"The trouble with that," Buchanan shot back, "is that it isn't my land. It's hers."

"Ah! But you know what's best for her! You can see the wisdom of the action I propose! Acting with her power of attorney—"

"Which I don't have."

"No problem! My lawyer can draw up the papers by ten tomorrow morning. You have Mrs.

100

Ford's confidence. You go to the hospital, have her sign it, return here to sign the deed transfer, and by noon tomorrow you can be preparing to be on your way."

Pilgrim had it all figured. Buchanan's pain had dulled his anger and replaced it with a clarity of thought that felt almost spooky. "And you offer what for the land?"

"Seven hundred and fifty dollars, sir."

"That's generous."

"I am a generous man."

Buchanan stubbed his cigarette in the big stone ashtray on his corner of the desk.

"Plus," Pilgrim added, "your commission."

Buchanan looked up. "What?"

"Your commission." Pilgrim gestured in the air. "Your . . . brokerage fee. Expenses. Call it whatever you wish, your payment for assisting in the completion of the transaction."

"And what—how much—would that be?" Buchanan asked softly.

"Does twenty percent—one hundred and fifty dollars—sound fair to you, Mr. Buchanan?"

It rocked him. For a few seconds, temptation was strong. He could take the money, solve all the problems, get Margaret back to Colorado, and have two months' pay in his pocket.

Pilgrim was watching him, a little smirk at the corners of his mouth.

Maybe, Buchanan thought, Pilgrim has never failed when he tried to buy a man off.

And that thought made his anger stir again.

Buchanan managed to get out of the chair. "I'll have to . . . think."

"Of course," Pilgrim said, coming around the desk, all concern and good fellowship again.

"Shall we say in the morning? About ten o'clock? Here in this office?"

Buchanan let him assume it if he wanted. "One of your goons took my gun."

Pilgrim hurried to the door and opened it. He said into the dark, "Which one of you has Mr. Buchanan's gun? You? There it is. Good. Thank you." He closed the door again and walked back, handing the Colt over butt-first.

Buchanan took it and put it in the leather. The room tilted slightly as he headed for the door.

Pilgrim preceded him and held the door for him. To the men outside he said, "Mr. Buchanan is not to be troubled in any way. Do you understand me? He and I have had a frank discussion. Let him go."

Buchanan pushed past him and out onto the narrow stairway platform. The men, bulky in the dark, stood back to let him pass. Buchanan limped past them and descended to the street below.

He walked a block, getting out of their view, before he stopped to examine his Colt. As he had suspected, the slugs had been punched out. He reloaded carefully. Then he walked through two alleys, hurting all the way, to assure himself that he was not being followed.

Finally assured of that, he made his way through the back part of town to the place where the giant log and timber bridge spanned the tumbling river. Nobody was around except for the man in the watchhouse, and by lantern light he appeared to be asleep sitting up.

Pilgrim had lied about Joe Ford. Surely he knew what Margaret had told Buchanan: Joe had been murdered.

And almost surely one of Pilgrim's men had been responsible.

There was more here than met the eye, some deeper plot by Pilgrim. How did it relate to the map Margaret had told him about?

Buchanan knew he had to have answers before he could do anything. But right now his pain made it impossible to think clearly, and the beating had taken all the strength out of him. *Hide. Rest. Figure it out later.*

He crept down the riverbank and slogged through mud to a place he found beneath the bridge where some repair lumber had been piled up, along with what looked a lot like wood shingles. Without making a sound, he created a little burrow in the pile and crawled in and was almost instantly asleep.

ELEVEN

Cold and pain woke Buchanan early.

Light rain was falling, leaking through the planks and timbers that formed his makeshift hiding place. Squinting through puffed eyes, he saw bleak pre-dawn light between the chinks overhead. He felt like every bone in his body had been broken.

Trying to ignore the agony it caused, he crawled out of hiding and got to his feet in the muddy slough beside the pile of lumber. The river boiled past him, the bridge formed a black canopy against the gray light overhead.

Examining himself, he decided that two or three ribs must be cracked. His mouth didn't work quite right because of swelling and the missing teeth, and he had little vision out of his left eye. His right knee was swollen and somebody had kicked him in the groin, judging by the way he felt down there.

Everything seemed to be working, more or less.

Climbing the bank of the river, he made his way out onto the muddy street, which was deserted. He walked west and then north, finding a few men out on the street here, and some of the stores getting an early start on what promised to be a dismal day.

After looking around a few minutes, he found

the store he wanted. The sleepy clerk was friendly and helpful, and seemed pleased to make a nice sale this early in the morning.

The next stop was a bathhouse on East Front Street. The proprietor either didn't know him or had been called off on Pilgrim's orders. He rented Buchanan his best bath stall.

The hot water in the wood tub felt marvelous, and he would have liked to soak more of the pains away. But time was pressing in on him. Using the razor on the shelf in the cubicle, he scraped the worst stubble off his face and examined himself in the mirror. The face of a beat-up stranger peered back at him.

After dressing in the new pants, shirt, and vest he had bought at the store, he carefully taped the newly purchased Remington .31-caliber double-action revolver to his calf above the point where his boot would reach. Then he pulled on the boots, jammed a dark blue wool cap on his wet hair, and left the bathhouse.

The sun was up, peering under a dark shelf of rain cloud. The clock on the courthouse showed 8:45 A.M. He hurried.

"Say, you're out early!" a familiar voice hailed him.

Turning, he saw Deputy Federal Marshal Pat Holroyd coming out of a cafe, a toothpick stuck between his lips. He waited and let the lawman catch up.

Holroyd scanned his face with narrow-eyed intensity. "You run into a haybaler?"

"You might say."

"What happened?"

"A couple of Pilgrim's boys jumped me."

Holroyd whistled and let out a soft, devout

string of profanity. "I don't have any jurisdiction at all inside the town limits, either, except in special circumstances. That goddamned sheriff is a corrupt bastard."

"No problem."

"Where are you headed?"

"A little personal business."

Holroyd's eyes narrowed again. "Look. You see now how rough they can play here. Watch yourself."

"Thanks." Buchanan turned away.

"Look," Holroyd called, turning him back. "I've got to go up into the Jocko Valley for a couple of days. I don't know how much help I might be anyhow, but I won't be around at all."

Buchanan studied the younger man's expression, liking him. "I appreciate your concern, Pat. Anything more you might do for us would only get you canned from your job anyway, the way I figure it."

Holroyd thoughtfully dipped a little snuff. "Not sure it's a very good job anyhow. You just be careful, you hear?"

"I hear."

"And if you need a friend while I'm gone, you might try Amos Moses, over at Moses Wagon Yard."

"You mean *somebody* around here isn't beholden to Pilgrim and his gang?"

"There are a lot of folks in that category."

"Not that I noticed."

"Well, you don't tangle with Pilgrim and his pals from the old Vigilance Committee, and most of the business community around these parts figure they need people like Pilgrim to make things grow. But he ain't universally liked, even if some

106

of the opposition sort of keeps its head down, if you get my drift."

"I think I do. It's maybe the first good news I've heard lately."

Holroyd studied him a moment and looked worried. "Well," he said then.

"This feller Amos Moses might have a horse for sale, you reckon?" Buchanan asked.

"He's got several. That's where I board my animal, and I saw his sale stock yesterday. He's got a couple of nice ones. Look. I'm on the way over there shortly. You want me to mention that you might come by?"

"I'd be much obliged," Buchanan told him.

"Done, then."

"Thanks." Buchanan turned away again.

"Be careful."

"Right." Feeling a little better about things, Buchanan trudged up the street toward St. Patrick Hospital.

"What time is it?" Lucas Pilgrim asked his attorney in the office.

"Almost nine," Jepton Laird told him. Laird was a youthful, florid-faced man, taller than the average, wearing a dark suit with a brocaded floral vest. He studied Pilgrim with slightly bulging, milky eyes that betrayed obsequious nervousness. "You're certain Mr. Buchanan will be here?"

Pilgrim smiled and watched his cigar smoke drift toward the ceiling. "He'll be here," he said smugly.

Buchanan found Margaret sitting in her tiny private room staring out at the drizzle, which had resumed as he arrived. The pale gray light of the

107

window softened her slender contours, made her face seem even more sad and beautiful. But as she heard his footstep, she turned and her smile was like sudden sunlight.

"Jimmy. Good morning."

He went to her. She rose and surprised him by embracing him briefly and brushing her cool lips across his cheek. She looked more rested, more calm. But her face tightened as she took in his injuries.

"What happened to you?" she demanded.

"I fell," he lied. "I'm fine."

"But—"

"There's no problem. Tell me, how are you today?"

She sat on the edge of her narrow bed. He took the straight chair. She said, "I feel a lot better—clearer. Sometimes I get . . . confused. But the doctor said that will pass."

"Good." He experienced a sudden rush of warm hope and gladness. "You look better already. You're safe here. Do what they say and you'll get better fast."

"I will."

"Margaret, I hate to bring up unpleasant memories. But about Joe—"

Her face changed, became frighteningly flat and withdrawn. "Where is Joe? Is he hunting?"

"What?" Buchanan absorbed the shock. "Don't you—"

"I really can't stay here long, you see. I have to get home to help Joe. Winter is coming on."

This pain was different from the physical, and felt worse. "Margaret," Buchanan said gently. "Don't you remember about Joe?"

"Will you visit us long?" she countered in the

same eerie, childlike tone. "Joe will be so glad to see you."

He grasped her hands, which were like blocks of ice. "Margaret. Please try to listen. I don't have much time. I have to find out some things. You told me about a map." He felt desperate, like he was wasting the precious time available to him. But he pressed on because he had to. "Do you remember the map, Margaret? Can you tell me what happened to the map? Because it might tell me a lot about what Joe was up to—what happened, why it happened."

"Of course," Margaret cut in in a different tone, but still frighteningly calm and detached. "I hid the map in the cabin, Jimmy."

Buchanan stared at her. Was *this* a moment of sanity? "In the cabin?" he asked, almost not daring to hope. "Where in the cabin?"

"Why, in the rocks of the fireplace," Margaret said with perfect clarity, as if she had never wandered from reality. "On the left-hand side, near the mantelpiece."

Twenty minutes later, Buchanan had found Moses Wagon Yard. Amos Moses greeted him warmly. He had two good horses in his small sale string, just as Holroyd had indicated. He made Buchanan a good price on a young gray mare who looked sweet and strong, capable of riding to Denver, if need be.

Moses didn't have any very good saddles, but he let Buchanan have his best for a price that seemed low, too. He threw in the blanket and bridle.

"You're losing money on me," Buchanan protested as the rotund older man helped him with the saddle strap.

"Pat told me about you and Pilgrim," Moses said, aiming a stream of tobacco juice into the corner of the stall. "Any enemy of Pilgrim's is a friend of mine."

"I thank you."

"Be careful," Moses said most seriously.

Riding out, Buchanan wondered how he could be careful and yet hurry, as he now knew he must.

He headed east for the Ford cabin.

TWELVE

Standing in the back of the Royal Flush Wagon Yard with some of Lucas Pilgrim's other hired guns, George Shue felt a crazy elation begin to build in his head.

Sometimes Shue realized that his brain didn't quite work right. He had spells sometimes when he blacked out for a few minutes. Most of the time nobody noticed, but he couldn't remember what had happened. Other times, the excitement filled him and he knew he was bigger than anybody, more dangerous, capable of changing the world or striding across the mountains or killing anybody for the sheer, hot joy of it.

He had killed several men when he felt like that. It always felt good, like sex.

Now, although the elation was recognizable as something that often preceded the killing joy, Shue felt in control, very controlled and cunning and happy. He was sure that at last *this* was his chance to prove to everybody how great he was.

He had the stranger, Buchanan, to thank for it.

Five of them were standing around, talking: Shue, Davis Enderly, Shorty Washburn, Henry Slater, and Jake Murnan. They had just seen Lucas Pilgrim's reaction when it became apparent that Buchanan was not going to show up for the

111

meeting with the lawyer, as expected, and it had been memorable.

Pilgrim had remained jovial and confident until more than thirty minutes past the time Buchanan was supposed to show. Then he had begun to scowl and pace, puffing a cigar with increasing anger. It was almost an hour after the appointed time when the attorney, Laird, took out his pocketwatch and studied it.

"Mr. Pilgrim, I don't think he's coming."

"Of course he's coming! I made him a fair deal, and he has no choice!"

Laird said nothing more, little glints of nervousness in his eyes.

Another twenty minutes later, Pilgrim turned angrily to Washburn. "Shorty. Go take a look-see around town. Davis and Jake, ask a few of our friends if they've seen him."

The men left. Shue and Henry Slater waited in the back of the office.

Pilgrim paced, his face getting more like a thundercloud.

Davis Enderly was the first one back. He reported that Buchanan had had a bath and bought some new clothes and an old revolver and ammunition. Pilgrim's face darkened.

When Jake Murnan came back to report the purchase of a horse and saddle, Pilgrim's temper broke.

"Somebody sold him a horse and saddle? Goddammit! Doesn't anybody have any brains around here?"

Murnan's eyes were round with fright. "It was Moses. But you sent us around, Mr. Pilgrim, to tell ever'body it was awright, nobody had to give him no more hassle—"

112

Pilgrim kicked a chair. It crashed against the wall, making everyone jump. "Where is he now? Why isn't he here?"

The door opened again and Shorty Washburn hurried in, sweaty and red-faced. "Archer McPride seen him riding out of town, going east."

Pilgrim, in the midst of knocking over another chair, swung around to face the much smaller man, and a remarkable change came over him. He trembled, and then all obvious sign of his mounting rage was gone.

He went pale. His face became monolithic and unreadable. The eyes with which he swept the room were like silent, deadly gunfire.

Even George Shue froze and stood very still.

But Shorty Washburn was too excited.

"I *knew* it was wrong to let the bastard go!" he panted. "We should of whipped up on him some more and th'owed his butt in the river. You messed up this time, boss, when you thought—"

Pilgrim moved so fast that Shue couldn't see exactly how he did it. All he knew was that Pilgrim's body seemed to explode. *Something*—maybe Pilgrim's fist, possibly his elbow—crashed into Shorty Washburn's face. The smaller man rocketed backward as if he had been shot out of a cannon, hitting the corner of the desk and a chair and slamming into the wall.

In the same silken movement, terrifying for such a big man, Pilgrim was astride him against the wall before anyone else could react in any way. He jerked Washburn's Colt out of his holster and swung it in a tight, vicious arc. The barrel slammed across the side of Washburn's face. Blood spurted. Pilgrim swung the gun back the other direction, slashing Washburn another savage blow.

For just a second, Shue was sure Pilgrim was killing Washburn. The gun barrel hammered into the side of the small man's head a third time, dashing him backward against the wall in a spray of red.

Then, just as suddenly as he had sprung, Pilgrim stopped. He held the gun ready to strike again. Miraculously, Washburn was not unconscious, although he was nearly so. He looked up, dazed, at the man towering over him, and blood fountained from his nose and mouth.

Pilgrim stood and tossed the gun onto the floor with a heavy clunking noise. He turned his evil eyes to the others in the room.

"All right," he said in a voice that was eerie in its calm. "Mr. Buchanan has not learned his lesson. Other lessons will have to be applied. Mr. Laird, thank you for being here. You may leave. When I require your services, you will be notified."

The lawyer gathered up his folders and scurried out of there.

No one else moved a hair. It was so still that Shue could hear his own breathing and Murnan's stomach growling. On the floor, Shorty Washburn made bubbling sounds as he tried to stanch the blood with his fingers.

"Get him out of here," Pilgrim said. "Patch him up. You'll all go to the Flush and wait. I have some things to check out, some thinking to do. We'll be riding back to the home place shortly."

Shue could not contain himself. "What about him?"

"About who?"

114

"Him. Buchanan."

Pilgrim's gaze bored through Shue's skull with shocking force. Shue felt like his head was being penetrated by invisible fire. He had never seen rage like this, or felt this kind of power. *Christ, he's going to do it to me now.*

Pilgrim said, "He's dead meat. Now get out of here. I have to think."

They had been happy to go. Now, standing in the wagon yard, they had stopped the worst of Washburn's bleeding. He was dizzy, pale except where the blood still splotched his face, but game. He was lucky to be alive and he knew it. They all did.

They babbled in the aftermath of the violence, acting like nothing had happened to Washburn.

"Did you see the way he looked at ole George?" Henry Slater asked reverently, his one good eye wide. "I thought *you* was dead meat, George!"

Davis Enderly surveyed the yard with cool withdrawal. "I wouldn't want to be Buchanan. Not now."

"What do you suppose we'll do?" Jake Murnan demanded.

"Hunt him down!" Shorty Washburn said, his voice a little thick. "Kill him!"

"I never seen him like that afore," Slater said, and shivered.

"I never want to see him that way about *me*," Murnan said.

The men looked at one another, together in their shared experience, and in their private suspicions. Was Pilgrim's rage spent? Would he decide one of them was to blame? It had been a very near thing for Shorty, and they all knew what had happened to Bert Atkinson, and to Lester LaSario

115

before him. So each man was thinking roughly the same: *Will he figure I'm to blame . . . put these other fellers onto sending me to hell like Bert and Lester?*

Every man was sweating and a little chilled at the same time.

But Shue felt elation as well. He knew he was not to blame. He also knew this was his chance to solve a mighty big problem for Lucas Pilgrim, and become his number one hand once and for all. . . .

In the upstairs office, Pilgrim finished his cigar. He finished thinking about meanings and alternatives. He formed conclusions.

He decided to let his anger cool further before taking action. There was too much at stake to make another mistake in judgment. Everything in him wanted to strike, and now. He could wait a little while . . . perhaps only hours. *Prudence!*

He walked out of the office and down the outside steps to the street. He had business at his ranch and business at the mine. Then he would make his final decision about dealing with Jim Buchanan.

It was afternoon by the time Buchanan reached the cabin. Wind sighed through the high firs, a lonely sound. He wondered if you heard the lonely wind when you were dead like Joe Ford, planted on a hillside under chunks of dirt and rocks and pine needles.

The cabin was undisturbed. He first found the balls of yarn and fishline he had spotted earlier, and went back outside with them. Using his pocketknife, he rigged a number of flimsy support stakes and put them into the soft ground all around the cabin, stringing yarn around them as he went. It was easy but slow and back-aching work. By the time he had run string from key points in the periphery alarm system, and hooked the strings to his tin cans precariously mounted on balance sticks near the front door of the cabin, it was getting on to evening.

In the evening light he couldn't see the thin stakes or yarn lines at all.

A Sac and Fox had showed him the trick. The brave had said critters sometimes tangled in the line and set the cans tinkling their warning, but wild animals almost invariably saw or sensed the line as an obstacle and stepped over it, low to the ground as it was. Even a horse ridden by a man would clear it nine times out of ten.

A man crawling up in ambush never would get over it without setting it off.

With the system set as well as he could set it, Buchanan made sure his horse was tied on a long grazing line, brought up some water from the creek, and went back into the cabin. Dark was coming fast. He lit a lantern, turned the wick high, and carried it to the hearth wall. He began examining the stones to the left of the fireplace.

All the stones looked solid and in good order. Holding the lantern closer, he examined them more carefully. Had Margaret been hallucinating? It was a dismaying thought.

But an unnecessary one.

Two rocks from the far left corner of the wall, his probing fingers detected an irregularity in the mortar that the eye could not see. The mortar was *crumbled.* Bits of mortar dust, and tiny fragments, came away with his fingertips as he felt between the rocks.

Leaning even closer, he made out the fine crack between two of the rocks.

Pulse quickening, he got out his knife and inserted the blade into the hairline crack. The rock stirred. Emboldened, he dug deeper and heaved out with his fingertips.

The chunk of granite started to slide out of its place.

Moments later, he had the rock in his hands and was lowering it to the horizontal portion of the hearth. Then he held the lantern up again, saw something inside the cavity where the stone had been, and plunged his hand inside.

He came out with a soft, much-folded piece of age-darkened leather. Spreading it out on the table under the light of the lantern, he studied it in amazement.

"Margaret, you weren't crazy this time," he breathed. "And by God, Joe Ford, maybe somebody had reason to kill you after all!"

It was only mildly cool in the night and Buchanan slept outside, wrapped in canvas against the rock foundation of the cabin. Nobody came to set off his tripwire alarm. He slept badly anyway, listening for it, hurting, and wishing for dawn.

The new day came clear. Buchanan ate some canned tomatoes and drank boiled coffee, and had his horse saddled before the sun was over the ridge. He scanned the surrounding terrain, making sure he had his bearings. The survey showed no signs that he was being watched, although he knew he could not be sure of that. He swung into the saddle, paying a price in the protest sent by his cracked ribs, and started off.

The crude leather map was clear about landmarks. He made good time. Within an hour he had found the creek that dissected the drawing, and followed it.

He didn't know where the map had come from. The way he had it figured, Joe Ford had come into possession of it and had followed it, just as he was following it now. Maybe Joe had followed to the end of the trail, to the place marked by the X. More likely, Buchanan thought, someone had intercepted him, killed him for the map, but somehow not found it. Possibly Joe had managed to hide it before he died, and Margaret had subsequently located it. For all anybody could know from present facts, Joe might have had the map memorized. It might not have left its hearth hiding place since before his death.

The map—and whatever it led to—might be exactly what Lucas Pilgrim wanted so badly.

Getting nearer the marked spot, however, Buchanan ran into a complication in his theory. He had clearly left the confines of the Ford property, and was either on someone else's, or on government land. That fact made Joe's possession of the map less easily explainable. And if the X was on somebody else's land, why was Pilgrim so anxious to get the Ford property?

There wasn't time to try to figure it all out now. Buchanan's horse followed the stream around a sharp bend where it tumbled into a narrow gorge, raw granite cliffs looking down on a brush-clogged flat and the water rushing white over boulders and smaller rocks. Erosion had done its work over centuries here, and the craggy rock walls were pocked with shelves, break-offs, and the black holes of countless natural cave entrances. The sun was high enough now to heat Buchanan's face and body. He started to sweat in the cool air.

A little later he came to an outcropping marked on the map. Just ahead, tamaracks and spruces formed a densely wooded backdrop on the hillside to the left, which sloped more gently here. The trees and brush extended to within a dozen yards of the stream, bounded by rock fields. On the right, the cliffs went up as steeply as before. A great rock seemed precariously balanced about two hundred feet up. This was clearly marked on the map, as were the higher shelf and the little waterfall.

And this was the point of the *X*.

Pulse quicker, Buchanan swung out of the saddle, tied the horse to a young willow, and walked through the fist-sized rocks of the bank to the waterfall. Wiping his forehead with his arm, he studied the map again. The *X* was clearly *in the water*, at the point of the fall.

He moved closer to the water's edge and studied the waterfall. Spring melt made the water run deep and swift. He couldn't see a thing. He thought about getting in and wading. But he didn't have any idea of what to look for, and the water was so swift that he knew he would have a hard time staying on his feet. At another time of year, this place might be almost gentle. At present—he looked downstream from the falls—the stream was only about two feet deep, but it was rushing so fast that a man who lost his balance in it would be carried around the bend thirty yards away and into God-knows-what.

Sharp disappointment filled him. He had come for nothing.

He stepped up onto a man-sized rock at the edge of the waterfall and strained for a better look.

At that point the voice rasped behind him: *"Now I got you, you bastard."*

Shocked, Buchanan started to turn.

"Don't you move, boy, or I kill you right now!"

He recognized the burry voice. Dismay hit. He had been a real fool, getting so engrossed in what he was doing that he let himself get drygulched again.

Very slowly, he turned only his head to peer in the direction of the voice.

George Shue, his face split by a leer of triumph, crouched perhaps ten feet away on the rock field between the creek and the trees. He had a Winchester repeating rifle trained at hip-level, and the mad light in his eyes said he would use it on any provocation.

"What do you want?" Buchanan demanded, his mind racing over possible courses of action.

"This ain't your land. This is Pilgrim land."

"I didn't see any signs or fences."

"Don't matter! You're trespassin'."

"I'll get off. Is that what you want?"

Shue's crazy eyes became slits. "What chew want here? What chew think you're gonna find here? How'd you know to come here?"

"Is it a special place? Is something important here?"

"Bastard!" Shue hissed. "I thought maybe I'd take you back, but it don't matter, does it? Mr. Pilgrim is real sore. *Real* sore—you should see what he done to Shorty—an' he's gonna be real

121

happy when I bring your dead ass in over the back of my horse."

Buchanan felt a chill to the bone. The dwarf-like gunman was not going to be talked out of anything—nor tricked out of position—and he was trembling from head to foot with a sick excitement, a killing lust. Buchanan was seconds from death.

"Get down from there," Shue ordered. "I don't want chew falling in there, gettin' carried downstream—"

He got no farther, because Buchanan's mind heard what he said. It opened the only chance to him, and he acted instantly on instinct.

He jumped backward as hard as he could propel himself.

"What—?" Shue screeched, and fired.

The slug spanged an inch from Buchanan's head, and then he hit the water. It was total, icy shock. The splash obscured everything and he lost his breath and then came up, pulled by the incredible force of the current. A bullet slammed into the water inches from his body and he got the briefest blurry glimpse of Shue, running along the bank, levering the rifle and firing again. Then the powerful force of the water bashed him over rocks and past a boulder and in under the snagging branches of a fallen tree, then sideways and wrong-side up again. It was chaos as he fought for breath, and the stream plunged him along, bouncing on the bottom and surfacing in spray and foam that obscured everything.

122

THIRTEEN

The force of the current carried Buchanan down through a rushing area of worse white water, crashing blindly off boulders and stickups, and into a deeper swirl on the curve where he was driven down . . . down . . . until all he saw was murky dark and he was sure he was going to drown. Then he was hurled up again, fighting toward air, and he popped out of the water, gasping and coughing, and turned around two or three times and got his bearings.

The stream had borne him around the bend, out of George Shue's sight. Here the current slowed, narrowing but deepening, with more of the rock field on his left, the cliffs almost to the edge on his right. Ahead he saw why the water was slower and deeper: a rockslide had tumbled massive boulders into the stream, forming a broken dam that almost closed off the flow across much of its width.

The current, still strong, carried him headlong into the big boulders. He slammed into one of them and managed to hang on.

He had to hurry. Shue would be hotfooting around the bend in pursuit.

Pulling himself up onto the boulder, he ignored the pain in his chest to clamber onto the next rock, and the one after that, swiftly making his way to the right-hand bank. He was soaked, frozen, a little dazed. But he knew he had to get away. Scrambling onto the gravel bank, he looked around for a way out, or a place to hide.

Brush choked the base of the cliff. Just above his position about fifteen feet, two layers of granite shelving overhung a series of man-sized holes, little caves.

There was no place else. He plunged through the brush, grabbed a handhold in the rock face, and climbed. There were handholds everywhere, a lot of the rock rotten with age. Desperation added strength. He climbed up and got his arms over the lip of one of the cave entrances, then pulled himself up and, with a final convulsive effort, fully inside. Once there, he rolled frantically downhill for about six feet and encountered the rear wall of the hole.

Gasping for air, he lay still for a few moments. Everything inside him hurt. He had hit something in the stream, and had a thin trickle of blood seeping down his face along with the water. Cold chills attacked him.

In a minute or two he began to get his wind — and his bearings.

The cave he had climbed into was small. The rock ceiling was about three feet over his head as he lay against the solid back wall. The mouth, circular, five feet in diameter, shone hazy-bright in the dark slightly above his head. He could see well enough to tell there was no way out except via that hazy halo of light. But out there somewhere was Shue.

Buchanan had his breath by now, and needed to know what was happening outside. He crawled carefully up the slight incline to the mouth of the cave and cautiously peered out.

For a few seconds he didn't see anything unusual, just the brush below his hiding place, the stream with its natural rockslide bridge, the field of rocks and trees on the far side. Where the hell was Shue?

Then he saw him, and got a shock.

The little man had been swifter than he anticipated. He was below Buchanan's position, laboring along the edge of the stream, *on this side,* having already crossed over.

He was moving along the bank, studying the rocks and brush with intense interest.

As Buchanan watched, Shue—almost directly beneath his cave—stiffened as he found broken places in the brush that betrayed where Buchanan had left the stream. The little man's head started to jerk up to scan the face of the cliff. Buchanan ducked out of sight.

"Buchanan?" Shue's voice came clearly, *"I know you're up there, boy. You can't get out. I got chew."*

Buchanan lay very still, even his breathing shallow. He knew his situation, and Shue knew it just as well: no way out the back, no way to climb higher on the rock wall with the shelves overhead—no way out except down, where Shue waited.

"I got lots of time, Buchanan. Lots of grub, a river full of water to drink. I can wait a lot longer than you can, boy."

Buchanan didn't respond. He was thinking about how long it was until dark, and what the chances might be then. Dull anger gnawed at his insides. Shue had every advantage.

125

There was no more sound from below. Buchanan forced himself to wait. The sound of the rushing water covered any other noises Shue might be making. Buchanan got his gun out of his holster and poured driblets of water out of the cylinder. He removed the bullets and wiped them dry with his hands as best he could, examined them, reinserted them in the chambers. The cylinder rotated freely. The action, gently tested, felt fine. The gun would fire—he thought.

After more waiting, his impatience grew and he had to risk a look outside over the lip of the cave. He stuck his head up cautiously, then drew it back in anticipation of a shot, got no response and raised it again slowly.

There was no sign of Shue below, or on the stream's other side. No sign of any kind of life.

Puzzled, Buchanan risked poking his head outside the cave to look up and down the cliff's face both right and left. He saw nothing. *What the hell?*

There were two reasonable explanations. One was that Shue was in hiding, waiting for him to make the mistake of revealing his position. The other was that the dwarf had hurried back across the stream to get his horse and supplies, in preparation for a long siege.

If that was the case, Shue might be gone another minute or two, and thus give Buchanan a chance.

If he was willing to take the risk of moving instantly.

Buchanan froze.

Was he willing?

He thought about being stuck in here for hours or days, finally being sweated out, a sitting duck.

Hell. Nothing ventured, nothing gained. And the devil hates a coward. And so forth.

Gun in hand, he sat up in the mouth of the cave, in clear view.

No response.

He swung his legs over the lip of the entrance, awkwardly turned around, and lowered himself to the face of the rock. His toes found holds. Holstering his Colt, he grabbed rock projections with his sore hands and started down just as fast as he could go, bits of rock tumbling around him.

He lost his grip partway down and slid the rest of the way, hitting hard in the brush at the bottom. The impact knocked the wind out of him, and he sat up in pain, fighting for breath.

Just in time to see Shue coming along the far side of the stream, walking awkwardly in the big stones and leading two horses.

Shue's horse, Buchanan saw with shock—and his own.

Shue led the horses to a sapling near the edge of the rock field, and tied his own horse there. He led Buchanan's animal down toward the water's edge. Puzzled, Buchanan continued to watch from the thick brush and weeds which made him invisible to Shue.

Shue stopped, Buchanan's docile animal standing quietly beside him. Shue scanned the rock face well above Buchanan's present hiding place. *"Hey, Buchanan!"* Shue called, wolfish teeth bared. *"I found your horse! You ain't going to need your horse anymore, boy. Can you see me, Buchanan? Watch this, Buchanan."*

The little man let the horse stand ground-tied, its reins hanging to the rocks. He took out his revolver. He aimed it at the horse's head. Buchanan understood only then with a bolt of horror. *Oh, no, goddammit!*

The revolver bucked in Shue's hand. The shot sounded hollow and distant over the roar of the stream. Blood and brains were blown out of the horse's skull and the animal staggered to its knees and fell over on its side with a final convulsive shudder.

Shue watched in fascination, then turned a fiendish grin up toward the cliff face. The sun shone fully on his features, which were twisted with a mad joy.

"Hey, boy! You see that? Just like I killt Joe Ford!"

Buchanan's rage swept through him, and then he felt cold, colder than he had ever felt in his life.

Without analysis, he stood from his hiding place in the deep brush, head and shoulders poking into the clear.

More than fifty feet across the stream, Shue did not see him for a flickering. Then he did. Alarm etched on his warped features, he started to turn toward Buchanan's unexpected position. Given his surprise, he moved swiftly, his gun coming around.

He was not fast enough.

It was a long shot for accuracy with a standard-barrel Colt, but Buchanan had practiced hundreds of hours during the years of his growing up.

And he was so revolted, so angry, that he felt like he could *will* the bullet home.

He fired twice.

The first shot took Shue in the chest. It staggered him. The gunman looked astonished. He continued to raise his own weapon in Buchanan's direction. That was when the second shot tore out his throat and hurled him backward like a rag doll.

Shaking, Buchanan clambered over the rockslide dam to the other side. Shue's form sprawled at water's edge, face up. Buchanan looked down into eggwhite eyes that would never see anything again. Then he put the toe of his boot under Shue's body and pushed him over with the strength of his revulsion. Shue rolled into the water, his clothes floating him. The current caught him and carried him downstream and out of sight around the next bend.

Buchanan briefly examined his dead horse, struggled angrily to pull the saddle and rigging off, carried them over to Shue's animal and set him free to find his way home. Then he heaved the saddle and gear onto his shoulder and started back the way he had come. But he didn't get far before he had to stop and bend over and retch.

After that he felt a little better, physically, and he shouldered his burden again and moved on. It was going to be a long, hard hike back to the cabin. But he had a hell of a lot to think about.

It wasn't just a matter of what he ought to do next, or how he ought to do it. The problem was that he had just killed a man.

When he had been a kid, a man named Hardin had paid a lonely winter visit to his hometown in Colorado, and out of their mutual aloneness they had struck up a strange and guarded friendship. Hardin, they said, was a gunman in hiding. He had shown Buchanan how to hold a revolver, spin it, draw it fast, shoot without consciously aiming. Then Hardin had vanished as mysteriously as he had come, but Buchanan had continued to prac-

129

tice until he was very good indeed . . . until the night in Gunnison when he had killed two men.

Buchanan had said then he would never use a gun again to settle anything. He had maintained his promise to himself until today.

Today, with George Shue, he had proven to himself that the skill remained, and that his noble promise has been self-deception. And he was sick at heart. A part of himself said he had been justified. Another part said he was a liar, a weakling, and a murderer whose hands now were no cleaner than those of the man who lay dead behind him.

And what in God's name still lay ahead now? Had Shue murdered Joe Ford on Lucas Pilgrim's orders, or from no more motive than the kind of madness that had made him kill Buchanan's horse? What was the meaning of the map? How was he going to do the best for Margaret—and deal with Pilgrim—and survive? Was he man enough, really, to do *any* of it right?

He was so buried in his reflections that he did not pay quite as much attention to the surrounding terrain as he had on the way out. So he did not see the distant movement in the woods behind him.

FOURTEEN

It was half past four in the afternoon when Davis Enderly rode back into the yard of Lucas Pilgrim's ranch, leading George Shue's horse. Shue's muddy corpse was tied across the saddle.

Word got to Pilgrim inside the sprawling ranch house less than one minute later. Enderly, with a ranch hand's nervous help, was still untying the ropes that held the body in place when Pilgrim rushed up, out of breath and livid.

"Is that Shue? *What happened?* He was supposed to be hunting."

Enderly's chill gaze swiveled around to meet his face. "Is that what he said?"

"He said he could bag an elk he saw nearby, we could all enjoy the steaks."

"He didn't go hunting no elk, Mr. Pilgrim."

"What *did* the idiot do? And what happened?"

Enderly explained. He had seen Shue out on the west range, and had started to pursue him with the idea of joining his hunt. But almost immediately it had become apparent that Shue was not headed for the elk range. On impulse, Enderly had followed.

He had been three miles away, on a mountain ridge, when Shue had accosted Buchanan. Too far away to stop it or interfere, Enderly had watched all of it happen through an old army spyglass he always carried with him.

131

Pilgrim listened with a mixture of incredulity and anger. "Shue had him cornered?"

"Yes, sir."

"I told him to leave that man alone for right now!"

"He must've thought he could be a hero or something." Enderly's cold eyes betrayed cynical amusement.

Pilgrim shook his head in disgust. "And Buchanan turned the tables."

"You might say. He shot shit out of poor old George. Good shooting, too. You can see—"

"I don't want to see," Pilgrim cut in quickly.

Enderly nodded and turned back to him. "Yes, sir."

"And you say this was at a waterfall on the Baldy side of the high ridge?"

"Yes, sir. Buchanan shoved him in after he shot him. I had to catch George's horse, then ride downstream and collect him where he'd hung up on a snag in the creek. Took a while."

"So you don't know where Buchanan went."

"No, sir. Last time I seen him was there at the falls."

"Off the high ridge," Pilgrim repeated carefully.

Enderly's expression betrayed his new realization that there was something significant here that he didn't understand. "Off the high ridge, yes, sir. Is *where* it happened important?"

Pilgrim, with a sinking sensation, ignored the question. "Come with me."

Enderly followed him into the ranch house. In Pilgrim's great, pine-paneled office a contour map of the area filled one wall. Pilgrim led Enderly to the wall.

"Show me the place."

Enderly did so. Of course he had no way of knowing that Shue's was not the first violent death to take place at the site. But Pilgrim did, and he felt like somebody had kicked him in the gut.

"Do we plant George out where the Mex cook is buried?" Enderly asked.

Pilgrim was thinking furiously. "No. You take him to town."

Enderly's chill gaze fixed on him as the gunman tried to understand. Pilgrim explained. Enderly's waxen expression changed to a smile.

It was late the next day when Buchanan got back to Missoula, riding on the back of a flatbed wagon driven by a farmer who had happened along while he walked the road back. He had stowed his saddle, bridle, and blanket at the cabin, slept in the woods, and then walked for four hours before the farmer and his skinny teenage son came along.

Light spring drizzle obscured all view of the nearby mountains. Missoula looked like a picture postcard that had turned dark in the sun. The farmer stopped his wagon near the big drygoods store on East Front, and peered back at Buchanan.

"This a good place, feller?"

"Perfect." Buchanan hopped out the back, walked around to the bench seat, and shook the farmer's hand. "I'm much obliged."

The farmer nodded and clucked to his horse, and the wagon eased away, wood wheels making cloppy noises in the sticky mud.

Buchanan, soaked through and chilled, made his way across the mucky intersection to the board

133

sidewalk and turned in the direction of the hospital. There were a number of men out despite the weather, mostly drovers and sheepmen, and here and there a soldier from the nearby fort. Buchanan wondered if Holroyd could be back from wherever he had gone, but figured it was unlikely.

It would have been good to know Holroyd was around. Buchanan didn't think Lucas Pilgrim would ignore him long; the land baron would have figured out by now that something bad had happened to Shue, and he would be taking other steps to eliminate the irritation that Buchanan represented.

Buchanan's plans were not elaborate. *Something* had been hidden at the waterfall once, and he was convinced that Joe Ford had died because of it. Pilgrim knew about it, or was responsible for Joe's death, or at least had a hint that something valuable had been around, and so he wanted the Ford land and any other land in that area.

Buchanan's suspicions leaned toward gold.

His knowledge of the local history was not deep, but he knew that gold and silver had been found in many places hereabouts. There were little mines all over this part of the country, and a few big ones. He knew there was silver over in the Coeur d'Alenes of nearby Idaho, and gold up on Cedar Creek. Over near Garnet they were taking out millions a year in rich gold ore. Some people said you might pan out a fortune in any river ravine, with luck, and that the surface hadn't been scratched yet on the deposits of sapphires and possibly other gems. Already one could find small mines, abandoned, here and there in the hills. But others were just being started, and people said the best stuff hadn't even been found yet. The Pend d'Oreilles had this legend, see, about a hidden valley so full of exposed ore that when the sun hit right on it . . .

Somebody, Buchanan thought, possibly had found a mother lode. The leather map still in his pocket either pointed the way to it or to another clue. Joe Ford had followed it up, and he had died as a result. Now Pilgrim was involved, but with what exact motives Buchanan couldn't be sure. Probably, in addition to wanting the land, he badly wanted the map. There might even be things on the map that weren't obvious, that Pilgrim might be able to follow somehow.

Yesterday's events—the walk back to the Ford cabin, a night of hiding out in the woods, and a day's trek through the cold drizzle with no food— had given Buchanan a roaring headache, among other things. He knew he looked like hell. It would have been nice to rent a bath and get some new clothes and put some hot food in his belly before seeing Margaret. But he just didn't think he could risk any of that. Even walking along the sidewalk, he felt exposed and vulnerable.

At least, he thought, no one could ever be sure about what had happened to George Shue.

The ungainly frame building that housed St. Patrick was just ahead. He crossed the street and walked up to it, and inside.

In the front office it was bare and gray, with no lantern or candle, but there was a stove burning somewhere; the building felt damp but warm. The waiting room was barren, only a chair and an old church pew, and a naked wood floor, but it felt better than outside. Buchanan rang the little bell suspended from a string and waited for somebody to come.

Within a minute or two, light footsteps sounded in the long corridor beyond the door at the far end of the room, and Sister Immaculata, carrying a washbasin and towels, appeared. She first smiled as she recognized Buchanan, but then she saw the condition of his clothes and her smile changed to a frown of concern.

"Mr. Buchanan. Have you had an accident?"

"Sorry about the way I look, Sister. I had to camp out last night and I haven't had time yet today to clean up."

Sister Immaculata's smile returned, dubious. "The weather is dreadful. Sometimes I believe what someone told me once, that summer here is one day in July."

Buchanan grinned dutifully. "Is Margaret doing all right?"

"She's doing *very* well. I was just with her. Dr. Stone is very encouraged, and so am I. Would you like to see her?"

"If I could."

"Yes. Let me tell her you're here, and then I'll take you back."

Buchanan waited. He was aware of a slight, pleasant tingling of anticipation. No matter what else might be going on, she had always affected him this way. He wondered if a lot of people experienced this welter of confusing emotions with the person they loved. It was so unique for him that he couldn't believe it was common.

Sister Immaculata came back. "She's glad you're here. Oh, and I warned her that you're something of a muddy mess at the moment. So she's prepared for that. We don't want her to experience any surprises that might frighten her, set her back."

"I understand."

Sister Immaculata frowned. "There is one other thing, Mr. Buchanan. I've discussed this with the doctor."

"Yes?"

"She isn't strong enough to talk about . . . the things that have happened to her. The death of her husband. Whatever may have followed. Even her arrival here. She becomes agitated when those subjects are brought up."

Buchanan felt keen disappointment. "I see."

"It isn't that she won't be able to talk about that part of her life one day, perhaps even very soon, with the remarkable recovery she's making. But Dr. Stone says—and I certainly agree—that she's very fragile now. Her control is very fragile and precarious, do you know what I mean?"

"I think so, yes."

"So we must ask you not to try to ask her about things that have happened to her in the recent past. Not just yet. Perhaps in a week or two . . . in a month or two. But now, talk like that could set her back totally. Do you understand?"

"Yes."

Sister Immaculata nodded with satisfaction. "Then will you follow me, please?"

Buchanan followed the nun through the door and into the corridor, then back into the rear portion of the building where the patient rooms were.

The sister's cautions should not have been unexpected, he realized, and they made sense. But he hadn't thought of them, and they radically changed his plans for this meeting. He had intended to ask more about the map, and about people who owned land adjoining the Ford property. Now he would have to get that in-

137

formation elsewhere, and he had no idea where.

Sister Immaculata took him past the cubicle where Margaret's bed was and all the way to the back of the building, where tall windows filled a barren sitting room with the gray light of the rainy day.

An old man sat slumped in a wicker rocker near the windows at the left. He seemed to be sleeping, a shawl around his bony shoulders. On the other side of the room, Margaret had risen from a similar chair, some knitting work tumbling from her lap to the bare wood floor as she moved.

She looked enormously better—more color in her face, her posture less strained and more graceful and natural, her hair loose on her shoulders. Her plain, gray dress hid the contours of her body, but she looked simply beautiful.

Her great eyes took Buchanan in an instant, and then, as he went across the room to her, she trilled gentle laughter.

"Oh, Jim!" she smiled, taking his hands in hers. "You do look awful!"

Her eyes were clear. She seemed totally sane and in contact. He squeezed her hands as relief flooded warmly through him. "And you look wonderful."

She moved close to brush her lips across the stubble on his cheek, then turned and pulled a straight chair away from the windows and close to her rocker. "Sit down. Tell me everything."

He obeyed, facing her so closely that their knees almost touched. "You first. Sister Immaculata says you're doing fine."

A little dark ghost went across her face, and then was gone. "I know how sick I've been, Jim.

138

The doctor is giving me medicine. It tastes awful and it upsets my stomach a little, but it makes my head clear. I still have . . . spells. But I'm going to be all right. I know that now. I feel safe, and I haven't felt safe like this for so long, not since Joe . . ." Her voice trailed off and the ghost scurried across again.

It was sufficient indication that Sister Immaculata's warning about discussing recent events was well-founded. Buchanan quickly changed the subject. "Tell me what the food is like here. And I see you're knitting."

Margaret accepted the change, and was her old self as she laughed about some of the food, and how clumsy she had become with knitting. She said she hadn't knitted since she was a child, crocheting being quicker and easier for making robes and blankets much needed in the household. Then she talked about Dr. Stone, and how much she liked him.

Buchanan realized there was a curious gap in her "normalcy." She said nothing about why he was here, what their circumstances were, how things might be at the cabin, nothing with significant substance. It was puzzling, but all he could do was go along and be glad she was doing as well as she was, with the hidden inner darkness far from exorcised.

He was beginning to grow uneasy, and anxious to break off this visit so he could assimilate her new condition and what it meant, when Sister Immaculata appeared in the doorway. She looked slightly strained and pale. "Mr. Buchanan?"

He took it as his cue. "I'll be back soon, Peggy. You're wonderful and you're getting better. Keep at it!"

139

Dismay at his departure clearly showing in her eyes, she hugged him briefly, intensely, and stood by her chair as he walked out.

Sister Immaculata had vanished. He walked up the long corridor, engrossed in his thoughts about the changes in Margaret's condition and what they meant.

He walked into the waiting room and found two men standing there. One of them was the deputy sheriff he had met his first day here. The other, also wearing a badge, was older, thickset, with wide-set eyes and thick beard. The sheriff.

Both men had their guns drawn and fixed on his chest.

"Buchanan?" the sheriff said. "You're under arrest."

FIFTEEN

Stunned, all Buchanan could think of was that any commotion here would terrify Margaret, so nearby. Shock trickled through him like icy sludge as Deputy Smith moved quickly beside him and snaked his Colt out of its holster.

"That's real nice," the sheriff said with quiet satisfaction. "Now I'll be much obliged if you'll hold your hands behind your back."

Buchanan obeyed, and Smith clamped cold metal manacles on his wrists.

The sheriff visibly relaxed, but kept his gun trained on him. "We'll just be going to jail, now."

Sister Immaculata appeared in the doorway to her office. Ashen, she had tears on her face. "Mr. Buchanan. I had no idea."

Before Buchanan could ask what the lawmen had told her—not that it would have made any difference in their ability to force her to bring him, unsuspecting, to the front—Smith prodded him from behind and he was led outside and into the drizzle.

No one spoke during the brief walk to the jail-house, a new, heavily constructed building next to the courthouse with a sign over the front door that said JAIL J.D. ABERCROMBIE, SHERIFF. Buchanan was badly startled and confused. He didn't speak until they were inside the too-hot jail building and Smith was unlocking a cell door.

"Sheriff, what am I charged with?"

The heavyset lawman gave him a sarcastic look. "I think you know."

"*What?*"

"Murder."

Buchanan was rocked. "Murder of who? When? How?"

"Shue. George Shue. Day before yesterday." Sheriff Abercrombie tucked some tobacco in his cheek. "An' I think you know how, mister."

It was totally unexpected. *How could anyone know?* Buchanan bluffed. "I don't know what you're talking about."

Abercrombie chewed reflectively. "Sure. Marvin, before we put him in the cell, search him. Search him real good."

Buchanan gritted his teeth and submitted to Smith's careful pat-down. The deputy's hands quickly found the bulge of his money belt under his shirt.

"What's this?" Smith pulled up Buchanan's shirt and pulled the money belt loose, tossing it to Abercrombie.

The sheriff unsnapped it and pulled the green-backs out. His eyes widened as he fanned the bills. "Helluva lot of money here. Where'd you get this kind of money, son? Have you killed some-body else we don't know about yet, and robbed 'em?"

"It's mine," Buchanan said through his teeth.

Humming, Abercrombie went to the desk, put the money in an envelope, and tossed it in a desk drawer. "Keep searching him, Marvin. No telling what else we're gonna find."

142

Buchanan fought to control himself. He knew how much chance he had of ever seeing a dime of his savings again. But even that seemed a remote concern at the moment. As Smith continued patting him down, he could only hope against hope that the deputy would get careless.

He didn't.

"Well, lookee here," he said with delight, pulling Buchanan's pantleg up to reveal the hideout gun taped to his calf.

"Killers got all kinds of tricks," Abercrombie said, and sent a stream of brown juice in the direction of the spittoon beside his desk.

Smith ripped the taped gun off Buchanan's leg with one motion. Buchanan flinched involuntarily.

"Don't hurt the boy, son," Abercrombie crooned. "We don't want to have to carry him up to the hangin' platform."

Smith finished the search. Abercrombie carried both of Buchanan's guns over to his desk and tossed them loudly into the bottom drawer. Smith shoved Buchanan into the cell. The door clanged shut and he twisted the big key in the lock.

"Fine 'n dandy," Abercrombie said with deep satisfaction. "Now what say you find one of Mr. Pilgrim's boys and let him know how good we've did, eh, Marvin? That's a boy." He spat again.

Darkness came. The sheriff vanished somewhere. Buchanan paced his cell, examining every inch of it and finding nothing that offered even the thinnest ray of hope. The walls were new, solid, thick. There was a window, but it was merely a slot near the corners about five inches wide and two feet tall, with a chunk of thick glass protected by a vertical bar that made it even more impenetrable. He could see the street, buildings beyond, the mountain beyond that. From his barred door he could peer down through the alcove that separated cells from the front office, but there was nothing to see except the lantern flickering on the corner of the desk.

He still didn't understand what had happened. Worry about Margaret, defenseless as long as he was in here, savaged him. Holroyd was the only other person he could count on. He tried to remember how long Holroyd had said he would be gone. A day? Two?

But even if Holroyd came right now, what good could he do? Federal law didn't interfere with the locals. And as much as Abercrombie reeked of corruption, he was the legal authority.

Buchanan clung to the hope that Abercrombie, for all his bluster, didn't really have a case. Shue's body must have been found, he thought, and Pilgrim had leaped to a right conclusion. But there wasn't any proof.

More of Pilgrim's patented harassment, he thought. The sheriff would hold him a few days and try to scare him into a confession. Then, when that didn't work, sooner or later . . . what? Would they let him go, hoping he had become sufficiently scared to leave the county? Or would some kind of jail "accident" be contrived, one that might leave him dead anyhow?

Evidence or no, he had plenty of reason to worry. For the next hour or two, that was just what he did, his headache worse, his belly sour and empty, and chills shaking him as his wet clothes refused to dry.

Deputy Smith finally came in, ushering a loud and profane waddie who was dead drunk. Smith

144

put him in a cell at the far end, and the rider promptly fell asleep. After leering in at Buchanan, Smith left again and Buchanan listened to the drunk's snores for a while.

Later, Smith came back again. He had a tin can of steaming soup and a chunk of bread that he passed through the bars. Buchanan was ravenous despite everything. He pitched in.

He wasn't quite through when he heard the jail doors open and close again, and more voices. Before he could sort them out, Sheriff Abercrombie came back through the alcove. Behind him was Lucas Pilgrim.

"This is the feller," Abercrombie said respectfully.

"Thank you, Sheriff," Pilgrim said heavily. "You've done good work. Now if I might speak alone for a moment with the prisoner . . .?"

Abercrombie nodded and shuffled back to the front office. Once there, he started making discreet noise with his desk drawers so Pilgrim could have some privacy.

Pilgrim, his long yellow slicker streaming water, removed his Stetson and let a thin trickle roll off the wide brim to the floor. His broad face was splotched with pink from the outside cool. "Filthy weather out there."

What the hell was going on? Buchanan didn't say anything.

Pilgrim moved closer to the barred door. "Mr. Buchanan, no one here wanted trouble with you. From the first, you've done nothing but antagonize me and violate legally constituted law in this valley."

"By not rolling over and playing dead for you?" Buchanan retorted.

Pilgrim's eyes flared, but he maintained steely control. "You should have come to the office to sign the papers, as I *thought* we had agreed."

"I must have got mixed up," Buchanan said. "I understood that was an offer, not an ultimatum."

Pilgrim lost control for an instant. He hissed, "By God, sir, call it what you want! If you don't cooperate, you're as good as dead around here!"

"And what are you here for now? To gloat, or what?"

Shaking slightly, the massive man regained his composure. "Whatever may have happened between you and Shue, Mr. Buchanan, I realize that George was a . . . mercurial personality, somewhat erratic and prone to pick fights—"

"He was crazy."

"All right. Have it your way. At any rate, I recognize that there may have been, ah, mitigating circumstances in his death." Pilgrim's piercing eyes went through Buchanan's skull as they had once before. "It is possible, if you show readiness to be reasonable, that this case will never have to go to trial."

"Meaning, if I get Margaret to give me power of attorney, and then sign the property over to you?"

"Wouldn't it be the simplest and best solution for all of us, Mr. Buchanan?"

"Let me tell you something, Pilgrim. I *know* now that you or your boys had Shue kill Joe Ford. I know there was something hidden out there on that creek. Maybe you've got it now, maybe you don't. But whatever it was, it made you sure you have to have all that land around there. What's out there, Pilgrim? Gold? Is that why you're so hellbent on getting the Ford land—

even if it means destroying a beautiful lady like Margaret, who never harmed anybody in her whole life?"

Pilgrim's eyes narrowed with a killing glare. "One thousand dollars for the deed. Another thousand dollars for yourself, and you can be out of here tomorrow and leaving Missoula on the Sunday stage."

"Goddamn you," Buchanan burst out. "Do you think I'd sell her down the river? I love her!"

Pilgrim stood more erect, his expression changing. "Ah. At last I begin to see. Of course a man would be a fool not to want her. She's beautiful. And there's a quality about her, a kind of vulnerable sadness—"

"But you'll never have her. And you'll never have that land. Not as long as I'm alive."

"Did it ever occur to you, sir, that you may not *be* alive much longer, unless you cooperate?"

"You don't have a case. You don't have anything but guesswork. If you did, you wouldn't be here, making this bluff without a card in the hole."

"You're a fool, Buchanan," Pilgrim snapped.

Buchanan hesitated an instant. This was the man who in all probability had killed Joe Ford, had virtually kidnapped Margaret, might even be partially responsible for her mania. *What all had he done to Margaret?*

Buchanan had never hated anybody the way he hated the hulking rancher at this moment.

Instead of replying in words, he gave Pilgrim an obscene hand gesture and turned his back on him.

Pilgrim's angry intake of breath was sharp and loud. "You'll regret this."

Buchanan leaned against the wall and stared out

through his tiny, useless window. When he finally turned back, Pilgrim was gone, and muttered voices in the outside office said he was conferring with the sheriff.

Even the whispers sounded angry.

An hour passed. Buchanan paced, trying to figure how long they could hold him without evidence. Wishing for a smoke. Then he heard the jail's outside door open again, and voices. In a moment shadowy figures appeared in the hallway between office and cellblock.

The first figure was Sheriff Abercrombie, holding high a lantern. Second was the hulking Pilgrim again. Behind him was an older man, silver-haired, florid, wearing an outlandish white suit and hat. The fourth man was one of Pilgrim's ruffians.

"Here he be," Abercrombie said, holding the lantern aloft so that it shafted bright light into Buchanan's cell.

Buchanan looked into Pilgrim's ball bearing eyes and saw the pleasure there. But Pilgrim was not doing or saying anything. It was his gunman who moved closer, peering in with all the appearance of nervous examination.

The older man in the white suit rumbled in a southern accent, "What do you say, Mr. Enderly? Is this the man?"

Enderly nodded vigorously. "Yes, sir, Judge. He's the one. I'd know him anywhere."

"Be sure, Mr. Enderly," the judge said solemnly.

"That's the man. He's the one."

"Very well, sir." The judge came closer to the bars. Close up, he had bloodshot eyes and a drinker's nose. The smell of whisky came into the cell with his breath.

"You are James Buchanan?" he intoned.

"I am. But what—"

"Mr. Buchanan, you are charged with murder in the first degree. How do you plead, sir?"

"I'm not guilty," Buchanan said, dazed. "What *is* this? What—"

The judge cut in, "You are entitled to legal representation, sir. The sheriff tells me you have money he took from your person. The court will appoint a lawyer and pay him out of your funds. Your trial will be three days hence, Monday morning, in the courthouse at nine o'clock."

"Trial?" Buchanan echoed. "What kind of law is this? *Who* identified me as doing what? Isn't there supposed to be a grand jury? A preliminary hearing or something?"

The judge's alcoholic face became more solemn than ever. "Mr. Buchanan, you have just been confronted by the witness who saw the heinous deed, the killing of one George Shue, late of this county, on the morning of yesterday. And you have just had your preliminary hearing, sir. I am hereby ordering you bound over for district court trial and held without bond."

Deputy U.S. Marshal Pat Holroyd's problem with cattle missing from the Flathead Reservation had taken him farther north in the Jocko Valley than he had anticipated.

Now, with dark spreading out over the Friday night sky, Holroyd sat cross-legged on the tent blankets with sub-Chief Running Wolf and two of his best braves. The smell of tobacco densely filled the tipi.

149

"My business here is done, Running Wolf," Holroyd said respectfully. "The two thieves have been caught, and I will take them back to Fort Missoula for a trial."

Running Wolf was young for his position of leadership, but his tough, cunning face showed why he had been chosen by Chief Charlo, and why he was said to be one of Charlo's favorites. "You say work done," Running Wolf grunted. "Men caught, fine. Our cattle stolen. Yet we are not allowed to try them by our justice."

Inwardly Holroyd sighed. It was an old story. "Running Wolf," he said patiently, "the white man's law must punish them because they are white men."

Running Wolf stabbed his thumb into his own chest. "But *my* cattle! *My* loss!"

"Justice will be done. You can come and testify if you want. I'll make sure you're notified."

Running Wolf's bitter expression deepened. "And one day they get your 'justice.' But our cattle gone, not found, sold someplace. Buffalo gone. Cattle stolen all the time. But we are 'good Indians,' huh? Because we don't make no trouble, just let you take our land, everything. Huh?"

There was no answer to the angry accusation. Holroyd knew just about everything Running Wolf said was God's truth. The Flatheads had always tried to get along with whites, accommodate them, move when asked to move, turn the other cheek. In return they were being ignored and wrecked as a nation.

Holroyd sighed again inside and tried to talk on with Running Wolf and his braves. He knew he couldn't do a thing, but at least he could listen. At least he could try to demonstrate that not all

150

white men were thieves and liars who didn't give a damn whether the Flatheads lived or died.

The palaver went on for hours, however. Holroyd stayed with it. He figured it was part of his duty. But any last thoughts he might have harbored about getting an early start back for Missoula were gone from his mind by the time he finally climbed into his blankets to sleep. The start would be late and with two prisoners in tow he would not make it back tomorrow—Saturday—as he had planned.

It worried him a little. He knew that his absence from Missoula left the man named Buchanan with no allies worth mentioning. But surely, he reassured himself, Buchanan wouldn't have done anything rash, and the time since his departure hadn't been long enough for Pilgrim to spring anything.

But Holroyd couldn't quite convince himself. He slept badly, tossing and turning.

151

SIXTEEN

The rain ceased in the night. Buchanan watched dawn come through the slit window of his cell. A few farmers and drovers appeared on the muddy street beyond the window, and an hour or two later—time was distorted in here, the way he felt like he was going crazy with apprehension—Deputy Smith came with some beans and biscuits, and then brewed rancid coffee.

Smith hunkered in the hall beyond the bars, well out of Buchanan's reach, while Buchanan ate.

"What for did you kill him, anyway?" Smith asked dully.

"How can you be so sure I did?"

"Hell! Davis Enderly *said* you did!"

"It's his word against mine."

Smith looked at Buchanan as if he were crazy. "Do you think there's going to be a jury picked here that'd take your word against his?"

"Is he that well known? That well liked?"

"He works for Mr. Pilgrim!"

"I guess I can hope the jury doesn't all think like that. They'll pick the jury on Monday?"

Smith looked startled. "Jury's already picked."

Buchanan felt a slight shock. "Already picked?"

"Sure. Same jury we used when we hung them four Indians a month ago. The judge liked that

152

jury. They got through the whole thing with him in less 'n an hour."

Buchanan digested this. "I guess somebody will have to hurry to get the gallows ready," he said, unable to keep the bitterness out of his voice.

"No problem," Smith told him cheerfully. "It's still up from the Indians, and the sheriff is going to check it out today, to make sure the trapdoor hasn't got rusted or anything."

It was almost insanely funny. "Good," Buchanan said. "We want to make sure every step of this thing is well-oiled, right?"

Smith blinked. He didn't get it.

The small wall clock in the hospital office had just chimed ten times when someone sounded the visitors' bell outside Sister Immaculata's room. She left her prayers and hurried to the front of the building to see Lucas Pilgrim and a much smaller man waiting. Both wore business suits and carried their hats in their hands.

"Sister," Pilgrim smiled, taking her hand. "It's good to see you again."

Something inside Sister Immaculata wanted to recoil from the touch of Pilgrim's hand, as if it were slimy and unclean. She fought the impulse to pull back. "Mr. Pilgrim. Welcome."

Pilgrim looked around the barren waiting room. "You've done wonders already, Sister. I see that my contribution was well used. If you require further assistance, I trust you will let me or my attorney here, Mr. Laird, know about it?"

Sister Immaculata nodded to the smaller man. "Mr. Laird."

"Sister."

She turned back to Pilgrim, and was conscious of starting to steel herself inside. "What brings you here today, Mr. Pilgrim?"

"You have a patient. A Mrs. Ford, I believe?"

The nun inclined her head in assent. Her heart beat a little faster.

"Mr. Laird and I," Pilgrim went on smoothly, "have an important business matter to discuss with Mrs. Ford."

"Oh, Mr. Pilgrim, I'm sorry, but she's much too ill to face the rigors of any talk about business."

"Of course, of course. How stupid of me. Well, then. Since I did care for her for some time after her husband's tragic demise, I'll just visit with her a few minutes, cheer her up."

Sister Immaculata was aware of her heartbeats now high in her throat. But her voice sounded calm. "I'm sorry again, Mr. Pilgrim, but Mrs. Ford is being allowed no visitors."

Pilgrim's color changed slightly. He was fighting anger. "On whose orders?"

"On Dr. Stone's, and my own."

"Surely you know I wouldn't harm her, Sister."

"Surely you know I do what is best for my patients, Mr. Pilgrim."

Pilgrim glared down at her, then jammed his hat on his head. "I'll be back."

Sister Immaculata watched the two men walk out of the building, across the board sidewalk, up the street. Pilgrim walked with great, long, angry strides, and his young attorney trotted along like a child in his effort to keep up. The nun's heartbeat was sickeningly fast and thick now that the confrontation was over. At some primitive, unconscious level Lucas Pilgrim frightened her more than any man she had ever known. If she had not

154

had her Catholic schooling and the church to teach her about such things, Pilgrim alone would have taught her about the existence of evil in the world; he reeked of it.

And he was not through yet, she thought with a chill. He was not only an evil man, but headstrong and stubborn. He wanted to see Margaret Ford. He would try to find a way.

Sister Immaculata shivered and hugged her arms around herself.

Voices in the outer office of the jail prompted Buchanan to sit up on his wood cot. Smith came back to the door of his cell, followed by a thin, pale man in a worn black suit with flecks of mud on his cuffs.

"Visitor," Smith said, unlocking the door. He swung it wide and the skinny man came in nervously, carrying a battered briefcase.

"Mr. Buchanan?" the skinny man said in a reedy voice. "My name is Hammond. The court has appointed me as your legal counsel."

Buchanan sized him up as they shook hands. The handshake was weak. Hammond's pallor bespoke illness. His suit hung on his gaunt frame and he could not have weighed much over 120 pounds. His eyes had a yellowish tinge to them. Hammond was not a man to inspire confidence despite his obvious nervous intensity.

Buchanan said, "Thanks for coming."

Smith banged the cell door closed. "Call when you're ready." He vanished into the office.

Hammond looked around the cell with some apprehension. "If we could, sit down, ah, Mr. Buchanan?"

155

Buchanan sat on the cot and motioned Hammond to do likewise. The lawyer balanced his case across bony knees and opened it. It was packed with dog-eared papers. As he shuffled them, a cough burst roughly from his lungs and suddenly became a fit. He bent, wracked by the seizure, his face going red.

Watching and listening, Buchanan felt his dismay grow. He had heard a cough like this before. The man had had consumption and had been dead inside six months.

With an enormous effort, Hammond got the dry, rasping coughs stopped. He wiped his mouth with a large linen handkerchief, already badly rumpled. Buchanan thought he saw flecks of dark blood on the cloth, but Hammond quickly folded the hankie and put it away again.

"Now, Mr. Buchanan, as to the charges. You are charged with murder in the first degree in the death of one George Shue, late of this county. At your preliminary hearing you entered a plea of innocence."

"They don't have any evidence."

"They have an eye witness, I'm sorry to say."

"But he works for Pilgrim, just like Shue did."

A film of sickly sweat appeared on Hammond's face. "Yes. Unfortunately, I have every reason to believe the jury will give credence to his testimony. Also, I understand that the doctor has removed one bullet from the deceased's body. It matches in caliber the bullets in your gun."

"There are a million Colts like that in this country!"

Hammond almost had another coughing fit, but caught himself. "Yes. Mr. Buchanan, we can go to trial with this case the day after tomorrow. But I

156

must tell you in all candor that I have little optimism about the outcome. On the other hand, there is an alternative."

Buchanan studied him suspiciously. "That being?"

"I have been led to believe that the special prosecutor named to present your case to the jury would look favorably on a bargain."

"Special prosecutor?" Buchanan echoed. "And who might that be?"

"Jepton Laird."

It struck him with a wild sense of inevitability. "Isn't he Lucas Pilgrim's lawyer?"

Hammond's eyes widened. "Why, yes, he may be, but—"

"Christ!"

"A bargain, Mr. Buchanan. A bargain *is* possible."

Buchanan fought to calm the anger. "What kind of a bargain?"

"If you were to plead guilty to manslaughter, the county would be saved the expense of a trial. In exchange, the prosecutor might be willing to recommend to the court that you be given a prison sentence, to be served at the new facility in Helena."

"And how long would the sentence be?" Buchanan couldn't keep the sarcasm out of his voice. "Life?"

"I believe the statutory term ranges up to twenty years, but—"

"Twenty years!"

"Perhaps less! Perhaps less!"

"Like hell." Buchanan was on his feet. "Why did they pick you? Because they knew you wouldn't fight?"

Hammond's face underwent a remarkable transformation. He went ice-white, and then stood to face Buchanan. "I don't fear these people, sir. When you have less than a year to live, you don't fear implied threats."

It was said so calmly, and with such force, that Buchanan immediately regretted saying what he had. "I'm under some pressure here," he muttered.

Hammond barked a little rueful laugh. "That's one way to put it. Look, sir. I'll fight this charge in court if you wish. There's no love lost between me and Pilgrim and his minions. They only let me have your case the way they'd throw a dry bone to a dying dog. And for appearances. But I have to tell you. You have a snowball's chance of winning. They'll ram the charge through, and you'll hang."

It was said with such simple sincerity that Buchanan chilled. It was the reality he had been trying to deny all night. "But," he said, "if I plead to the lesser charge . . . ? What's to prevent them from double-crossing you?"

"I make sure that the charge is reduced before I hand in the signed statement by you, admitting the lesser charge. There's no death penalty for manslaughter. The *worst* they could do was try to give you a life sentence in the new facility at Helena."

"Life! Jesus!"

"I don't think they'll do that," Hammond said doggedly. "They say they won't. And at any rate," his eyes burned intensely as he looked at Buchanan's "you would be alive. You could appeal. You might . . . escape . . . one day."

"It's not a great alternative," Buchanan told him.

158

"*Any* alternative is good when the other possibility is the gallows."

Buchanan sank to the cot again. Gall choked him. He knew the young, fatally ill lawyer was talking straight. But he didn't know if his own pride would let him sign an admission giving Pilgrim his victory.

And what the hell would that mean to Margaret?

Abandonment.

But wasn't her cause all but lost already, unless he could somehow work out something with Holroyd to help her?

Your case is over, Buchanan. You've lost. It's just a question of how they rake in your chips.

It was the worst feeling he had ever known in his life.

He looked up at the lawyer, still standing. "I'll let you know," he said. His voice was thick, and, shockingly, his vision was blurry, like he was crying.

Hammond put a thin hand on his shoulder. "I'll come back tomorrow. We have to decide by then."

He turned and called to Smith. Buchanan sat on the cot, his face in his hands.

It was late Saturday when Sister Immaculata again heard the bell sound in the visitor room. She hurried to the front and found Lucas Pilgrim standing there once more, again with his lawyer.

"Mr. Pilgrim," she burst out, "we're very busy here. We have confessions this evening, and—"

"This won't take long, Sister," Pilgrim said, a glint of triumph in his evil eyes. "I have come to see Mrs. Ford."

"I told you—"

The lawyer interrupted her by thrusting a long, legal-sized piece of paper at her. She stopped, took it, and began, with a sinking sense of horror, to read it.

"As you can see," Pilgrim told her, "this is a court order, a restraining order, to be exact, which legally forbids you from interfering with my right to see Mrs. Ford. You *must* let me see her now. Where is she?"

Sister Immaculata looked up from the paper and tears bolted from her eyes. "Oh, sir! Don't do this! Please! She's so ill, so weak—she can't *stand* any tension yet, any reminders of the things she's suffered."

"Nonsense," Pilgrim said easily, pushing past her. "All we want to do is have her sign one small paper. Now where is she?"

The distant, tinny sound of a church bell signalled Sunday morning. Buchanan examined a cloudless day through the narrow slot of his cell window, and then resumed pacing.

Smith was late with breakfast. It hardly mattered.

For the second straight night, Buchanan hadn't slept more than an hour. His nerves were rubbed raw. His stomach ached, tied in knots. His face itched with a stubble beard and his head hurt. The earlier pains in his body, courtesy of the beating by Pilgrim's men, had changed to a nagging stiffness, a constant, pulsing discomfort.

None of that mattered much, either.

There had to be a way out of this, something he hadn't seen. He examined every inch of his cell

160

for what seemed like the hundredth time, found nothing, and paced some more.

He was honest enough to admit to himself that he was scared, badly scared, although he kept it under stern control. To die any way was bad enough. To think of dying by a hangman's rope was horrible.

He had seen a hanging once. The horse had been kicked out from under a sobbing, screaming killer and he had hit the end of the rope with a shock that jerked his body into the shape of a question mark at the same instant his neck was snapped. The man had flopped, then, twisted and kicked and spasmed, blood bursting from his face, and Buchanan had thought it was never going to be over and had turned violently away. Then, when he turned back, the limp figure swayed from the tree limb, a figure that didn't even look like a man any more.

They wouldn't hang him, Buchanan vowed. Maybe he would take the plea the lawyer offered. Maybe he would make them grind through the sham of a trial. Either way, there would be a chance for escape. And even if it wasn't a very good chance, he would try to take it.

He might die, but he would not hang.

Still, his insides turned over at the prospect. Not only would his death let Lucas Pilgrim win; it would leave Margaret abandoned. That thought hurt worst of all. He hadn't remembered how much he truly loved her. Not until he had been with her again. Now, to be so near saving her, possibly even winning her for his own . . . to have it all snatched away, to fail her and maybe die, knowing that —

He gritted his teeth so hard in frustration that

he started some of the bleeding from the beating again.

Some time around noon, Smith led another visitor back. Buchanan looked up, expecting the lawyer, hoping for Holroyd. He got neither.

"Mr. Buchanan." Sister Immaculata clutched the bars, staring in at him from tear-reddened eyes.

Smith said matter-of-factly, "Have to talk through the bars."

"You let Hammond in here," Buchanan said angrily.

"That was a lawyer. Sorry." Smith ambled back to the front.

"Sister," Buchanan said. "What is it?"

"I couldn't stop him, Mr. Buchanan," she choked. "I did my best. But then he got a court order."

Buchanan's guts hit the floor. "Pilgrim?"

The nun started to weep silently, her face hidden by the hood of her habit. Buchanan reached through the bars and grasped her chin, forcing her to look up. "Tell me!"

Sister Immaculata fought for, and found, some control. She gasped for breath. "Pilgrim. Yes. He came to see Margaret. I denied him access. He came back later. He had a court order. I couldn't disobey a court order. He went back. I ran for Father Mario. I don't know what they talked about, what Mr. Pilgrim and his lawyer said to her, but I was gone only a minute or two, and when I came back with Father Mario, we could hear her screaming the length of the building—she was screaming 'No! No!'—and we ran back there. Mr. Pilgrim had a legal document of some kind. Margaret was backed against the wall of the common

162

room. She was crying, holding her hands out as if to push him away."

"What was Pilgrim saying to her?" Buchanan groaned.

"I don't know. Father Mario told them to leave. There was a horrible row. Mr. Pilgrim was very angry. We finally got them out of there."

"And Margaret?" Buchanan demanded. "Did she calm down? Is she all right? Sister!"

"I'm sorry, Mr. Buchanan. She was . . . set back."

"Set back? Set back?"

"I don't know. Dr. Stone came last night, and he was with her again this morning after Mass. She—something Mr. Pilgrim did or said triggered her old memories. She—she wasn't making much sense last night or this morning."

Buchanan stared at her, feeling like the last of his world had collapsed.

"I didn't know whether to tell you or not," Sister Immaculata pleaded. "I didn't even know you were here until this morning. But you have a right to know."

Buchanan summoned everything inside himself to appear calm. "You did right, Sister. Now can you keep Pilgrim from seeing Margaret again?"

The nun's chin jutted. "Having seen the effect of one visit, I'll die before they see her again, court order or no."

"We're going to get all this straightened out, Sister. Stand your ground."

Sister Immaculata left. Buchanan attacked the cell wall with his fists.

"All right, sir," Lieutenant Slattery told Pat

163

Holroyd. "If you'll sign this paper on the bottom line."

Holroyd leaned over the guardhouse desk and scrawled his signature on the form which turned his prisoners over to the army. Then, after shaking hands, he limped stiffly out into the night.

The scattered lights of Missoula glowed nearby. He swung once more into the saddle and rode to the gate of the fort, then headed down the dirt road that led into town.

Holroyd was bone-tired. It was getting late. About all he wanted was a hot soak-bath, a shave, and a bed. The lights of Missoula's saloons, as he passed them, didn't hold any appeal. By the time he had neared the bathhouse, he decided even that could wait until tomorrow. He turned his horse toward the livery barn, thinking only of sleep.

At the barn, no lights showed. Holroyd dismounted thankfully, led the tired horse up to the closed front doors, and banged loudly on them.

"Come on, Amos, come on," he muttered.

After a minute, the yellow light of a lantern danced through chinks in the boards. The right-hand door swung open and Amos Moses, wearing only his longjohns, peered sleepily out at him.

"Sorry, Amos," Holroyd said, leading the mare inside.

"You just back?" Moses enquired, eyeing him sharply.

"Give her some extra oats," Holroyd said, and started to turn away.

"I guess you ain't heard," Moses said, stopping him.

"Ain't heard what?"

"That feller you said to do business with? The one that had a hassle with Pilgrim?"

"Buchanan?" Holroyd saw something coming, and braced inwardly. "What about him?"

"Seems like he killt George Shue." Moses spat. "Seems like he's in jail, and they're gonna try him for murder in the morning."

Buchanan sat on his cot, feeling his scabbed-over knuckles in the dark. Out front, a door opened and he heard voices.

"I know it's late," a familiar voice said, rising in anger. "But I said I want to talk to the prisoner."

Smith's crabby tone said something in reply, but then there was a scraping of boots and the flare of the lantern as it was turned up and carried in the direction of Buchanan's cell.

The light beamed in through the bars, almost blinding him.

"Be quick about it," Smith said irritably, and trudged back to the front, leaving the lantern on the floor.

Back-lighted, Pat Holroyd peered through the bars in weary disbelief. "So it's true."

"You've got to get me the hell out of here," Buchanan told him.

"They say you killed George Shue."

"Whether I did or whether I didn't—"

"Did you?"

Buchanan lowered his voice. "All right. Yes. It was self-defense—a fair fight."

Holroyd shook his head. "A hell of a lot of weight that's going to carry in this town."

"Listen to me," Buchanan grated. "There was a map. It belonged to Joe Ford. I followed it and

165

found a place where maybe something had been hidden. Then Shue jumped me. He got me cornered, shot my horse. I didn't have any choice."

"How do they know it was you?"

"One of Pilgrim's other men must have been trailing him. He says he saw it."

Holroyd shook his head again. "God almighty."

"Can you get me out?"

"It's not my jurisdiction," Holroyd said bleakly.

"They gave me a lawyer. Name of Hammond."

"Yeah. He's a lunger. Won't live long."

"He advised me to plead guilty to manslaughter. He said he could get me a term at Helena."

"What did you say?"

"I told him I haven't decided yet. I have to tell him in the morning before the trial starts, if I want to do it."

Holroyd's eyes were more bleak. "Are you going to do it?"

"I don't know about that. Listen. Pilgrim went into the hospital with a court order and talked to Mar—to Mrs. Ford. He got her all upset again. I'm sitting in here and going crazy. If you can't help me, surely you can go see how she is. Protect her from that son of a bitch!"

"Pilgrim forced himself in on her?"

"The sister tried to stop him but he had that damned order. Then he tried to get her to sign her land away or something and she cracked up again and I don't know if she is—whether she's all right. Pat! Whatever happens to me, you've got to protect her!"

Holroyd looked at the floor. "Jesus, you've really made a mess of this. All right, I'll tell you what. I'll go over there, see how she is, come back here, let you know."

"And you'll protect her from that bastard?"

"I'll do my best."

Buchanan breathed a deep sigh. "That's the first good news I've had lately."

Holroyd studied him. "I don't know what I can do about you. They've got it all stacked against you."

"That's all right. That's fine. Check on *her*."

"I'll be back."

Sister Immaculata was startled and frightened when the visitors' bell sounded so late. She was relieved when she found the deputy United States marshal, Pat Holroyd, in the waiting room.

"You startled me, Marshal."

Holroyd looked gray with fatigue, and grimmer than she had ever seen him. "I came to see about Mrs. Ford, Sister."

"For Mr. Buchanan?"

"Yes."

"I'm afraid she's still terribly upset by the earlier incident."

"You mean Pilgrim's visit."

"Yes. Dr. Stone says it's too early to tell how long it may take her to recover. You see, being brought here by Mr. Buchanan, seeing him again after whatever she went through, served as a sort of counter-shock, the doctor says. And she reacted wonderfully to being here. I think she felt safe for the first time in ever so long. Then, when Mr. Pilgrim came and put pressure on her to sign that paper, or whatever he did, it brought back all the earlier shocks and terrible memories."

Holroyd watched her through narrowed eyes. "And now she's acting . . . how?"

167

"She's withdrawn. She doesn't seem to know what's going on part of the time. When you speak to her, she may respond perfectly rationally, or she may say something out of her past that makes no sense at all."

"Damn."

Sister Immaculata sighed. "My sentiments exactly. If Mr. Buchanan can get out of jail and visit her again, and if we can keep Mr. Pilgrim away from her, then Dr. Stone thinks we can turn her around again and begin the task of rehabilitation."

"I don't think we can count on Buchanan," Holroyd told her.

The sister felt a pang of new worry. "The case is too serious to negotiate in some way?"

"I think if he would cave in and play ball with Pilgrim, maybe there would be some miraculous—you should pardon the expression—change in the charges."

"But Mr. Buchanan is not likely to do that."

"No. Which means, unless I miss my guess, that he's going to the gallows or the pen."

"Oh, no!"

"Yes. And then Mrs. Ford will be quite alone, and whatever game Pilgrim is playing, he'll win."

"We just can't allow that to happen!"

Holroyd's lip curled bitterly. "And how are we going to stop it?"

"I . . . don't know."

"I'll go back and lie to him, Sister. I'll tell him she's better."

"And then?"

"And then nothing. I'll attend the trial. Make sure it runs by the rules. But we both know who owns the judge and the jury."

168

"Oh, Marshal Holroyd," Sister Immaculata said, filled with dismay.

"Good night, Sister."

After Holroyd left, Sister Immaculata returned to her office but was unable to concentrate on her report to the bishop. She was filled with worry and remorse. Somehow, she thought, she should have prevented some of this.

She went silently, long habit rustling in the quiet, back to the patient rooms. It was dark back there. Margaret Ford's door was ajar. The nun stood still, listening to see if her patient was sleeping.

From the room came the soft, strange sound of *humming*.

Margaret's humming.

It was a childhood song, something like "Londonderry Air." And Margaret's voice sounded like a child's voice.

The sister risked peering in through the cracked door.

Margaret, in her long nightgown, stood at the faint light of her window. Looking out into the night, she continued to hum the happy, eerie little tune. Tears glistened on her cheeks.

Sister Immaculata went back to the front, and into chapel. She knelt in front of the statue of the Virgin.

Blessed Mother, she prayed, *tell me what to do!*

And almost like a miracle, the idea came to her.

But I can't! she thought, aghast.

Yet the idea grew and took possession of her.

* * *

169

The endless night had slipped past midnight, judging by the quiet stealing across the far end of the street where the jail was located, and Buchanan sat on his bunk, trying to think through a roaring headache. He had told Hammond, the lawyer, that he would plead guilty to manslaughter in the morning when court opened. Hammond had been vastly relieved.

"You're doing the right thing, sir."

Buchanan doubted it. He was steeled for the judge to give him the death penalty anyway, or a life sentence.

Pilgrim was going to have him out of here, one way or another.

Some time during the day's activity, however, Buchanan knew there would be a chance. Possibly a very thin chance, but a chance. He would watch for it and he would take it. He would either escape or be killed. Nothing in-between.

He was down to that bleak set of options.

When he heard the rapping on the front door of the building, it startled him. He knew Smith had long since turned the lantern to guttering low, and was softly snoring up front.

Buchanan stood and went to the bars, half thinking it would be some new gambit by Pilgrim or his people.

The tapping was repeated more urgently.

Marvin Smith rolled out of his corner bed, muttering, and got the lantern turned up. Yellow light flooded down the hallway. "Just a minute, just a minute!"

Buchanan heard him open the front door and say something rude. A soft voice, unidentifiable, replied. There was a moment's argument. Then Smith, still muttering, appeared in the door to the hallway, back-lighted by the lantern he had left on the desk.

Behind him came the slender, unmistakable silhouette of a nun.

"If you say it's an emergency, it better be an emergency," Smith complained. "Dadgum, never get a decent night's sleep around—"

He got no farther.

The nun's silhouette moved up sharply behind him and her right arm raised, then came down fast. There was a *thunk!* and Smith went to the floor like a sack of feed.

Sister Immaculata, still clutching a short length of pipe, bent over him. "Dear God! If I made a mistake and hit him too hard—!" Then she looked up and glanced at Buchanan through the bars. "No time for that now." She bent lower over Smith's unconscious form and pulled the key ring off his belt loop. She hurried to Buchanan's cell door and fumbled with the keys.

"It's the long brass one," Buchanan said, trying to handle his surprise.

Sister Immaculata inserted the brass key in the lock and turned sharply. The door sprang open.

"Run, Mr. Buchanan. Run for your life."

"Good God, Sister! You're going to be in so much trouble—"

"I've planned it," she said grimly. "You'll leave and I'll lie down on the floor and pretend that I was hit from behind, too."

"They won't believe you. You won't have any injuries."

Her eyes, although frightened, flashed with a trace of angry humor. "What will they do? Search me?"

Buchanan shook his head in wonderment and

briefly examined the fallen Smith. His skull was intact and there wasn't much bleeding. As Buchanan checked him, he groaned, about to come around.

"Where did you learn to sap a man like this, Sister? In the convent?"

"Hurry, Mr. Buchanan!"

He went to the desk, found both his guns and the envelope that still contained most of his money, and hurried out of the jail.

Outside, he stopped for an instant on the black, deserted street.

Now what? he thought.

SEVENTEEN

Pat Holroyd had just fallen off a precipice of sleep when the excited voices on the street a block away awakened him. They weren't your ordinary shouts, and it sounded like a gathering crowd, which meant trouble at this hour.

Groaning, he rolled out of bed, pulled on his pants and boots, and left his little house. Up at the corner, lanterns danced in the dark and a dozen excited men milled around.

"*Jailbreak!*" one of them yelled at him as he approached.

"*Somebody busted that killer out!*" another voice cried.

Everybody was excited and talking at once. More men were coming. A few had already saddled up and were ready to go hell-a-tearing somewhere. The horses reared and pranced nervously, adding to the general confusion.

Holroyd limped stiffly around the gathering crowd and approached the jail. Lights blazed inside. Two local toughs, temporary deputy badges reflecting light off their shirt, stood at opposite ends of the front porch. Both had shotguns.

"Hold it right there, buddy," one of them said to Holroyd as he approached.

"It's me," Holroyd said, and moved cautiously closer.

The lantern light fell on him and the new temporary deputy recognized him. "Oh. Sorry, Marshal. Come on up."

Holroyd went onto the porch. "What happened?"

The man rubbed his wrist across his face as if to clear his vision. His face was puffy and he needed a shave, and he might have been a little drunk. "One of them sisters came to see the prisoner. Late. Marvin started to let her in, but somebody banged her on the head, and him too, and used the keys to bust that feller Buchanan outta here."

It sounded about as likely as flying to the moon. Holroyd kept his face straight. "Who's inside?"

"Sheriff. Marvin. Judge. Doc."

"What happened to the nun?"

"Somebody took her to the hospital over yonder."

Holroyd thought he might have to change his theory. "She's that badly hurt?"

"Nah. She was lucky. Not hurt as bad as poor Marvin. She walked over there with an escort her own self. Them nuns live over there, you know."

Holroyd relaxed a little on that score, anyway. "What happens now?"

"Hey, I just work here. Sheriff deputized four of us for right now in case the fellers get outta hand. There's gonna be a posse, more deputized, but not until they look at their hole card in there."

"Thanks, pal." Holroyd went past him and entered the jail.

Three lanterns blazed inside. Sheriff J.D. Abercrombie bent over a map spread across the

174

desk. The judge hung over the map beside him. On the corner cot, a bleary-eyed Marvin Smith sat in obvious pain while the doctor finished wrapping wide bandage material around his skull.

Abercrombie looked up. "You're here. Good. We need all the help we can get. That murderous fiend had help from outside—busted out. We're fixing to go after him."

"You know which way he went, then?" Holroyd asked.

"Not yet, but Hector was awake over in the bridge house, and nobody crossed thataway. I figure he either went north or east, maybe out toward Hellgate. I'm going to put some men out on all the roads. Somebody'll spot him sooner or later."

"A man can hide out in these mountains for a long time."

Abercrombie gave him an angry glare. "I know that. I wasn't born yesterday. But I'll tell you what. It's still getting durn cold at night. He's got no supplies and no food. Either the discomfort will drive him down to town again, or he'll have to hunt or steal some food and we'll get lined out on his whereabouts."

Holroyd thought about it. "What can I do to help?"

Abercrombie's eyes squinted with suspicion. "Ain't you a pal of his?"

"I stopped some killing, probably of innocent people, when he took that woman out of Pilgrim," Holroyd replied. "The way I hear it, you've got a solid case of murder against him, with witnesses. If you want help running down a killer, I figure my job is to help. If you don't, I'll mind my own business."

175

Abercrombie appeared mollified. "Tell you what you can do. You can let 'em know out at the fort what's going on. And since you always seem to get along with some of these worthless Indians, you can spread the word with them, too."

Holroyd let the slap at the Flatheads pass. "I'll do that, then."

Dr. Stone straightened up from his work on Marvin Smith. "That ought to do it, Marvin."

"My head hurts like fire," Smith whined.

"Take it easy for a day or two."

Abercrombie said irritably, "He ain't taking it easy. His stupidity caused this ruckus. He's going to lead the posse that searches east."

"I guess you'll just hurt then, Marvin," Stone said cheerfully, closing his bag and starting for the door.

"Where now?" Holroyd asked him.

"I'm going to check on the sister."

"I'll walk you over there."

More men had gathered on the street outside the jail. Lanterns swung in the dark, and a couple of pitch torches blazed with crimson smoke. Missoula hadn't had such excitement in months. There was too much noise for Holroyd and the doctor to talk on the way to St. Patrick.

At the hospital, an older nun, Sister Chastity, met them in the visitor room. The old nun looked pale and frightened, and said Sister Immaculata was lying down.

"I really think I better check her injury, Sister."

The old nun hurried fretfully away, and in a minute or two Sister Immaculata, still wearing her full habit, appeared in the doorway. Her nervous eyes went from Stone to Holroyd and back again.

"He got away?" she demanded huskily.

Stone ignored the question. "I'd better check that head wound, Sister. Where the unknown assailant," his tone deepened with possible irony, "struck you."

"No, no. I'm fine. Just a headache."

Stone eyed her speculatively. "Still, I ought to examine you."

"No. Really. I've examined myself."

"Examined yourself?" Stone's skepticism showed.

"With a mirror," Sister Immaculata said lamely.

"I see."

"The blow barely broke the scalp. Presumably my habit cushioned the blow. There was very little bleeding, and that has subsided. I'm sure I'm just fine."

"And," Stone said heavily, "you're feeling no after-effects?"

"No."

"No dizziness? Nausea?"

"No."

"Disorientation?"

"No, thank the Lord. I feel quite all right."

"I see." Stone looked at Holroyd and started for the door. "Thank you, Sister. If you begin to feel after-effects, you'll send for me?"

"Of course," Sister Immaculata said calmly.

Outside, the doctor said to Holroyd, "You believe that cock and bull story?"

"Of course," Holroyd told him. "Otherwise, what explanation for Buchanan's escape could there be?"

"Of course," Stone agreed after a beat.

They walked to the corner and separated.

Holroyd went on, walking north and out of the street commotion near the jail, considering his options. There was no doubt in his mind that Sister

177

Immaculata had faked her injury and had sprung Buchanan. He wondered how much good that would do in the long run. Unless the Coloradoan was willing to fork a horse and ride straight through the mountains, never looking back, his troubles were far from over. And with the Ford woman still in the hospital, Holroyd figured there were two chances of Buchanan's fleeing: little and none.

Holroyd was wide awake again now, and his own headache said sleep would be impossible. He decided to go to the livery and ride to the fort at once, doing what he had agreed with Abercrombie to do. Might as well look motivated. After that, he could keep tabs on things, and if and when Buchanan showed up somewhere, try to prevent a lynching. He did not look forward to it.

He reached Moses Wagon Yard. He had his own key to the little Judas gate in the double front doors, and quietly used it to enter.

A lantern hanging from an overhead beam guttered low, casting the faintest illumination over the stalls that held several horses, the straw-covered floor, the ladder to the hayloft. The door to Amos Moses's sleeping room was closed tight, and the faint sound of lusty snoring penetrated the partition.

The back door of the barn, the one that led into the corral, stood ajar about six inches.

Holroyd's scalp prickled.

He looked carefully up the black ladder hole into the hayloft.

Then he said quietly, "It's me. Holroyd. I'm coming up."

He climbed to the top of the ladder and peered out over the ocean of hay clogging the loft. Sitting halfway back on the right hand side, Jim Buchanan stared back at him.

Buchanan experienced intense relief. "Come on up," he said quietly.

Holroyd crawled over and sat beside him. "You're not out of the woods, pardner."

"Tell me some more news."

"Why didn't you take a horse and hightail it?"

"Because Smith woke up and started screaming bloody murder before I was two blocks away. I ran to the first place I could think of where they might not look right away."

"Well, they're still milling around down there. But Abercrombie is going to form up two posses, and before long this county is going to be crawling with trigger-happy deputies."

"I don't know what to do about Margaret," Buchanan admitted. "I don't know what's going to happen to the nun."

"She broke you out?"

"Of course."

Holroyd smiled and nodded. "I thought so."

"Have they figured that out yet?"

"No. One thing you can count on with Abercrombie is his stupidity."

"Good."

"That doesn't mean he isn't clever. He's like a possum. Low brain power, but long on cunning. He takes a real bad view of you being out, and he'll deputize drunks and would-be vigilantes all over this part of the country if need be, to run you to ground."

"I need time," Buchanan told him. "I've got to get back to the place marked on that map I told

179

you about. I've got to search for some clue to what was there—and might still be there, for all I know."

"Then what?" Holroyd demanded.

"Then I confront Pilgrim. He's the one behind all this. He has the answers."

"He'll have you killed on sight."

"Margaret is never going to have any peace until I find out what's so precious out there that he would destroy her to have her land."

Holroyd frowned over it for a moment. "Well, I don't have time right now to figure out if you're right or wrong. All I know is, this place is going to be swarming with deputies after a while. If you have any chance of getting out of town, it's right now."

"Where to?" Buchanan asked.

"I'll explain while we saddle up."

They climbed down the ladder and started saddling. Amos Moses was awakened by the commotion, and started out of his sleeping room. When he saw Holroyd and Buchanan together, his eyes widened enough to show that he realized at least part of what was going on. He turned without a word and went back inside his room and closed the door again.

Holroyd chuckled as he jerked the cinch strap tight. "He's a good man."

"You know how much trouble you're in if we get caught together?" Buchanan asked.

"A shitload," Holroyd grunted, swinging into the saddle. "Come on, friend. Let's get out of here."

They rode out, following an alley north and

quickly putting the town behind them. It was a stark, clear night. No moon shone, but the illumination of a million bright stars made the countryside pale and perfectly visible. The night cold sank into Buchanan's skin and then into his bones, and he shuddered from it, his teeth chattering. There was nothing to do but keep moving.

Nobody challenged them. They moved across some open grass and then along a ravine line, staying as close to the trees as possible. They didn't talk.

After a half-hour or so, Holroyd nudged his mount toward a gully area with hills as a backdrop. They rode through heavy brush and then standing firs and pines, picking their way across some fallen lodgepole pines that beavers had taken down. The roar of water came closer and then they came out beside a narrow, fast-rushing stream with wide, round-rock banks on both sides. Holroyd led the way as they paralleled the stream for a while, then came to a very wide and shallow place, trees to the waterline on both sides, no sign of ripples, where they waded all the way across.

More time passed. Either Buchanan began to warm up from the exercise, or he became numb to the cold. He couldn't tell. They worked through woods, gradually climbing, and then down through a valley and on to another slope. They were beginning to get into the mountains.

Another hour passed as they rode switchbacks, climbing. The horses worked hard, their breath coming in jets of steam. Somewhat below them now, the scattered yellow lights of Missoula and a few other lights at the fort broke the velvet black of the valley. It was hard to imagine all the frenzied activity that must be going on down there.

181

Finally, still another hour later, Holroyd reined up. They had come out onto an outcropping along a switchback. On one side of them was the bulk of the mountain, which loomed straight up another three thousand feet; on the other side was a drop-off to a shelf of woods a thousand feet below. Beyond that was blackness, and far beyond that blackness somewhere, the now-distant lights of Missoula.

"I'm turning back here," Holroyd announced. "You work your way on up. There are a few little caves. Near the summit there's a big-ass bare rock shelf, with the grandpa of all pines standing just on the downslope side of it. Mark that spot. I'll meet you there tomorrow night a little after dark, or as early as I can get there. I'll have some chuck in my saddlebags for you."

"I've got to get to that spot marked on the map," Buchanan told him.

"I know that," Holroyd said patiently. "But just lay low for one day, all right? Let some of these fair-weather soldiers wear themselves out a little. Let me see what's going on, bring you some fresh information. Then we can go from there."

Buchanan looked at him in the faint starlight. "We?"

Holroyd looked surprised. "Yeah," he said finally. "I guess so. I never was very smart." He turned his horse downslope, leaving Buchanan alone on the mountainside.

For the second time in less than a week, Lucas Pilgrim was roused from his ranch house bed in the middle of the night. Standing in his gigantic dining room, only two of the hundred candles in the huge chandelier burning, he faced Henry Slater with mounting rage and incredulity.

"And he got out *how?*" Pilgrim demanded.

Slater's one good eye blinked furiously. "I'm just telling you what we was told, boss. One of them nuns went in to visit, and then somebody hit her on the head, and Marvin Smith too, and busted him out."

"And he's *loose* right now?"

"He was when Enderly tole me to hightail it back here and let you know what's happened. Sheriff's gettin' up a posse—"

"And they can start looking for one icicle in a blizzard," Pilgrim rasped, knocking over a chair.

Henry Slater clutched his hat and didn't say another word.

Pilgrim prepared and lit a cigar with hands that shook. He saw instantly that the nuns had somehow found the audacity to break Buchanan out. He should have anticipated that, after the scene with Immaculata and the priest—all that just because Margaret got a little excited. *Damn!* And now Buchanan was on the loose again, heading God knows where.

It could not be tolerated.

No more.

Pilgrim had tried negotiation. It hadn't worked.

He had tried intimidation, with similar lack of results.

He had thought the murder charge would be a nice, neat ending.

But now Buchanan had messed that up, too.

Only one thing could be done now, Pilgrim thought. He simply could not tolerate any more interference from Buchanan or anyone else. He needed only the Ford deed and two others now. Nothing could be allowed to get in his way.

It was time for direct intervention, a simple and brutal frontal attack on the problem, and its solution. And for that, what did he have to do? How could Buchanan be maneuvered?

Almost the moment the question came clear in Pilgrim's mind, so did the answer.

It was dangerous, but he knew it would work, and he liked it. It was foolproof.

He turned to the one-eyed Slater and said in a shockingly controlled voice, "Get back to town. Send Enderly and Murnan. You're to stay in town with Shorty for the time being, and watch. Before you head back, go to the bunkhouse and find Baxter and send him up here to me. We need to change some of the ranch security arrangements. Hurry, Slater, damn you! I want Enderly and Murnan back here right after sunup!"

Slater scurried out. Pilgrim mentally reviewed his plan, and a thin smile cracked his lips. Perfect. He should have done this in the first place. His mistake had been in trying to be too nice.

EIGHTEEN

By noon on Monday the weather had turned cooler, with clouds riding in out of Canada, threatening rain. The low gray of the sky shut Missoula in, making the air dense, suffocating.

Two groups of horsemen, five in one and seven in the other, had been out searching for the escaped killer since two A.M. A rider from the east group had come back a little before noon, getting some camp supplies. Nothing had been heard from the southwest group yet, but Sheriff J. D. Abercrombie had sixteen more men waiting to ride in relief when some of the fair-weather deputies wore out and started straggling in.

Nothing like it had happened in Missoula since its founding, and every saloon crackled with excited talk and loud boasting about what each man would do if he got the man named Buchanan in his sights.

At the jail, Henry Slater faced Sheriff Abercrombie. "Just so it's *writ down*. Not just said."

"I wrote it, I wrote it," Abercrombie said testily. He hadn't had any sleep and he was nearing the end of his patience.

"Mr. Pilgrim," Slater insisted stolidly, "wants to be *sure*."

"You gave me the list of the men he wants

deputized," Abercrombie cut in. "I gave it straight to the judge and his bailiff is going to enter it in the record. They're deputized. *Now*. You and the rest of 'em."

"Awright," Slater sighed. "I just want to make sure."

"You can be sure."

"No word of anybody seeing him yet?"

"Not hide nor hair. A man could hide in these mountains a long time."

"With the five hundred dollar reward Mr. Pilgrim put up," Slater said, "I figger folks'll look real hard for him."

Bending over his area map, Abercrombie ignored the comment.

Slater went outside, looked at the clouds, sniffed the air. Over in front of the town's biggest drygoods store, several riders were carrying out canvas and slicker material in order to have them ready when they rode out and the rain came. Slater didn't think it was going to rain. He thought the skies were going to clear up.

The storm that was coming was of a different kind, he thought.

He walked to the North Star Saloon and found Shorty Washburn and Jack Maxville standing at the bar, nursing beers and working to destroy the rest of the free lunch. Washburn's face was black and blue from the brief, savage beating he had taken the other day. Maxville, younger, rail-skinny, with sky-colored eyes that gave Henry Slater chills, looked remote and watchful.

"Where is he now?" Slater demanded.

"Across the street, in the federal office, still," Washburn said.

"You're sure?"

186

"We're sure," Maxville clipped. "No back door to that building."

"All right," Slater said. "I'm going to the livery to check on the horses."

"If he rides out," Maxville said in the same cold tone, "he'll have to saddle up too. We'll have plenty of time to get ready to follow him."

"I just don't want to leave anything to chance. I want to be ready ahead of time."

Maxville's thin smile was condescending. "What's to worry about?"

"I just want to be *ready,*" Slater repeated nervously. "And if you don't know why we ought to worry about screwing up," he added, with another glance at Shorty Washburn's face, "then I ain't going to try to tell you."

Maxville began building a smoke. Slater felt another chill. He left the saloon and headed for the livery barn, worried.

The newest man on Pilgrim's elite force, Maxville had been trailed to the Montana country by two stories of his killing efficiency that had made a couple of the boys smile and wet their lips, but had filled Slater with foreboding. Slater was no angel, far from it. But this emergency marked the first time Maxville had been assigned mainline duty, and Slater considered it bad luck that he was the one assigned to partner the gaunt teenager.

Maxville, he thought, was the kind of crazy who always made sure somebody died in a crisis. What worried Slater was that Maxville was not the kind who worried too much about who the victim was.

Their job was to follow Holroyd if he left town, plain and simple. And if Pilgrim's suspicions were

187

right, and he led them to Buchanan, Pilgrim wanted him taken alive, for the hangman.

Slater didn't think Maxville would exercise much restraint in order to take somebody alive, if push came to shove. And he didn't think Buchanan would go gently, either. Slater found himself hoping that other parts of his boss's risky scheme paid the dividends. If he and Maxville ended up following Holroyd and finding Buchanan, he thought somebody was likely to end up dead. And as crazy as Maxville was, the dead gent might be anybody.

"You and Murnan will handle the job itself," Lucas Pilgrim told Davis Enderly. "Baxter will drive the carriage."

Davis Enderly nodded coolly. "Understood."

"There can't be any slipups."

"There won't be."

"And she must *not* be hurt. If she's hurt in any way—"

"She won't be," Enderly said.

"All right. Of course, if Buchanan is found by nightfall, we don't do this."

"Yes, sir."

"You'll be in town. You'll make that judgment."

"Yes, sir."

Pilgrim sighed. "Fine. Explain it to Murnan and Baxter, and get moving."

Enderly left the ranch office, his spurs clinking softly on the carpet. The door closed behind him.

Pausing to light a cigar, Pilgrim walked to the wall of glass that looked out from the corner of the sprawling ranch house. A few hands were cutting and branding in the big pen a hundred yards downslope, toward the three tall barns, the horse corrals and tree-lined garden field. Far beyond these the sun was trying to break through the low clouds to glint silver-white on the high snow remaining in the mountains. Trees tossed in the breeze, and in the distance eagles swung against the sky in relentless search. Spring. Everything unsettled.

As unsettled as Pilgrim felt in his gut.

Goddamn her! he thought with a rush of emotion. *I did everything for her. She didn't have to go all to pieces and make this happen.*

It hadn't been his fault, exactly, that her stupid husband had had to be killed, he thought. And once that had happened, he had moved as swiftly as he could, when he got back from Arlee, to make sure she was sheltered, cared for, protected. He had even had the decency to provide the job in town, rather than simply taking her into his house, to give her the appearance of independence.

He had done everything imaginable to help her heal. He would have waited months longer, if necessary, before forcing the issue about the deed to that damned land.

All because she touched something in him that no woman had touched for so long. Feelings like tenderness. Longing. A sharp, insistent tug in his loins as the sheer physical desire for her waged war with the desire to treat her properly, show he cared about her, win her love.

But what had she done? Gone downhill into worse mental illness, bouts of more severe withdrawal and depression. And *still* he had been patient, had waited.

He couldn't wait any longer.

189

Buchanan had seen to that.

Thinking of the tall man from Colorado, Pilgrim was filled with impotent rage. What right had he had to barge in, take her off, probably sleep with her—*oh, Jesus!*—and then take her tearful kisses, her adoration, her gratitude for *nothing*, and put her in that hospital with those simpering, disgusting, holier-than-thou nuns.

Well, all right. Pilgrim had tried everything to do this the easy way, the legal way, to spare her. Now his hand was forced. There would be no more gentle measures.

His plan now had several facets, and only one was dangerous to her. She would just have to bear it as best she could. He was through waiting. He would have her. Now. He would have the land. Now. Buchanan would be destroyed. Surely within two days' time.

It felt good to know that the shilly-shallying was over.

At the hospital, Dr. Stone came into Sister Immaculata's office after examining the patients. "Mr. Litwhiler is better. I think he just had some gastritis."

"And Margaret?"

Stone shook his head.

"The same, then?"

"Actually she was better again for a few minutes. Then she lapsed."

"She doesn't know what's happened with Mr. Buchanan."

"No, Sister, and she mustn't. Her mind has taken too much. I think each of us has some level, some saturation point, beyond which we simply can't take any more grief or fear or anger. Her point was passed. But if we can keep her quiet, the setback from seeing Lucas Pilgrim—whatever they fought about—may be healed with time."

Sister Immaculata turned her long, waist-belted rosary in her pale hands. "I worry about her very, very much."

"Sister," the doctor said, "so do I."

In the afternoon, from his hiding place high on the side of the tree-covered mountain, Buchanan saw the riders move along the valley floor far below him. They turned and followed the Bitterroot toward the west. Later, two Flatheads, on foot, appeared farther up the slope of the next mountain to the west, but they too were far away.

Buchanan ate some berries and drank out of an icy stream. And waited.

Hours later, the sun slanted low in the west. In the valley below, the faintest haze of woodsmoke gathered over the cluster of houses and buildings that was Missoula. Buchanan could strain his eyes and make out riders on the road between downtown and the fort, and horsemen inside the fort itself.

Nearby, woodchucks scurried through fallen leaves and pine needles. A squirrel came close and watched him with brightly expectant eyes. Crows called alarm and a redtail hawk swung across the clearing sky. A vast silence reigned. The stirring of the high wind in the oldest trees was constant, echoing, modulating itself in tempo with the settling in of cooler air as the sun continued to descend.

191

Night came, and with it the cold. The instant the sun was gone, he was chilled to the quick.

Not daring a fire, he moved downslope from his hiding place to a spot in the deep brush overlooking the barren rock slab marked by the enormous pine Holroyd had set as their meeting place. He hunkered down, worrying about Margaret, fretting because Holroyd was so late.

A high cloud haze obscured the stars and made the night black.

Two hours passed.

Where was Holroyd?

Buchanan told himself to stay calm, not borrow trouble. He risked a smoke, cupping his hand around the cigarette to hide the glow from distant observation. The feeble heat of the cigarette warmed the inside of his hand and made him shiver more, realizing by comparison how cold the rest of him was.

A long time later, he heard the sounds of a horseman approaching: slow hoofbeats on hard dirt or rock, the brushing of the animal's body through weeds and underbrush. He stayed hidden, gazing toward the approaching source of the noises. Whoever was coming, he was making no attempt to be quiet. It sounded like he was even making more noise than necessary. That boded well. Holroyd would do that for him.

And after a few more minutes, a horseman appeared out of the woods below the rock shelf. He moved his mount up close to the shelf, in full view, and dismounted. Letting his horse stand ground-reined, he made a smoke, the flare of his match sharp in the blackness.

Smoke swirled in the dying glow of the match.

"Jim?" the shadow called softly.

Relaxing a little, Buchanan stood and moved out of hiding. His boots made clunking sounds on the rock shelf as he moved closer. The shadow stiffened its posture.

"It's me," Buchanan said.

The shadow relaxed and became Holroyd as Buchanan walked up to join him. "I was worried. Christ. Not that there isn't all hell to pay already!"

"Is that why you're late?" Buchanan demanded. "What's happened?"

"Where's your horse? Your other gear?"

"He's tied up in a little rock draw along the side, there, and up about two hundred yards. And all my gear, except for the saddle, blanket and bridle are on my back. What *happened?*"

"I don't like standing out here on this naked rock. Let's start up there and I'll tell you."

Buchanan turned and waited for him to gather his horse's reins. Then the two of them walked off the rock shelf and started climbing in the dark through the trees.

"It's bad," Holroyd said grimly. "Don't go crazy when I tell you."

"What?" Buchanan rapped.

"A couple of hours ago, somebody broke into the hospital."

Buchanan stopped dead in his tracks at the edge of a rocky washout that had made him detour on the way down. "Margaret. What happened to her?"

Before Holroyd could reply, there was a sharp, quick movement out of the darkness on Buchanan's right, and at the same instant on his left, about twenty yards away on either side.

"Don't move!" a voice clattered.

Buchanan's reaction was instant and without thought. He spun and dove headfirst into the rock washout.

A gun blasted orange fire behind him and a bullet hit flesh. Holroyd's horse screamed and reared up and Holroyd jumped away from it. Then Buchanan didn't see anymore; he hit the bottom of the washout—rocks and dirt ten feet down—on his head and shoulder.

Up on top in the blackness more gunfire erupted, two or three different guns, five or six shots.

"I got that one!" a man's voice yelled shrilly.

"Shut up! Shut up!" another man shouted.

Spitting dirt and blood, Buchanan twisted his Colt out of the holster and scuttered along the bottom of the washout, clambering over big boulders and crunching through smaller rocks. The wash shallowed just ahead—he had walked through that part of it on the way down—and he went to his belly to crawl up the side and get a quick look at the scene of the ambush.

Silence had fallen over everything. Overhead, the night clouds had broken in a jagged line, and starlight shone through, suddenly bathing the earth in a feeble silver light that looked as bright as day to Buchanan's night-quick eyes.

There was a rustling, kicking sound—something scrabbling in rock and loose dirt—and then the noise of Holroyd's horse whinnying in terror and pain, panting as it struggled.

Buchanan peered over the lip of the rock wash.

In the starlight, the horse lay on its side twenty paces away, back legs jerking spasmodically in death throes. What looked like black grease pumped in a tiny, ugly fountain from its neck.

194

Beside the horse, a body sprawled on the ground. By the hat that had tumbled beside the fallen figure, Buchanan recognized Holroyd.

Two men walked up to Holroyd from opposite sides, one tall, thick, shambling, the other painfully lank, moving with a will-o'-the-wisp grace. Both had guns drawn.

"It's not him," the thicker figure said hoarsely.

"He's here," the other man said in a shrill, staccato voice. "He ain't gone far." He raised his voice, neck craning, and yelled, *"Buchanan!"*

Buchanan lay in hiding, holding his breath. In the light it was an impossible shot, even for him. The gun was slippery in his hand.

The skinny figure shrilled louder, *"Buchanan!"* His voice echoed off walls and rocks and trees and across the valley, coming back ten times.

The thicker figure said nervously, "He's gone."

"Fuck, he's gone. He's not gone." He raised his voice. "Buchanan! I know you can hear me, you son of a bitch! Listen! You come out right now, or I kill your partner!"

With that, the skinny man leveled his right arm, revolver extended, at Holroyd on the ground. Holroyd was conscious—he moved involuntarily, bracing himself.

The thicker man said huskily, "You can't do that, Jack! Jesus!"

"Shut up! Shut up! I'll do what I want! We want Buchanan, right? We don't care about this sucker! I'll kill him! I'd like to kill him! *Buchanan! You hear me? Come out or I kill his ass!"*

Buchanan felt his insides shrivel. He hesitated, weighing the odds.

In the total silence came the sound of the

195

skinny man's revolver being cocked. It was the ugliest sound in the world.

Buchanan licked dry lips. "Hold it!"

Both standing men froze.

The skinny one called, "You come out! Now! Or—"

"I'm coming," Buchanan rasped, and climbed out of hiding.

From the skinny man came a high, nervous giggle. "There he is! You see? You see? We got him! Come over here, you bastard. Hold your hands high."

Buchanan obeyed. He climbed out of the wash, got to his feet and walked across the partial clearing, pine needles soft under his feet, his Colt in his upraised right hand.

The thicker man stood stock-still, training a gun on him. The skinny one moved toward him with the shocking speed of a snake. Buchanan didn't have time to react. The skinny man's arm swung and the barrel of his revolver crashed into the side of Buchanan's skull, dropping him to his knees in a shower of yellow stars and a cloud of pain.

"Don't try to hang onto that piece with me, you shit!"

Buchanan's gun had dropped somewhere. The skinny man—closer up he looked like no more than a wild-eyed, insane kid—stood over him, lank legs spread. Buchanan had blood in his eyes and couldn't focus well.

"And don't try no other tricks," the skinny kid hissed. He moved again and the barrel of his revolver slashed across Buchanan's face, knocking him over backwards in a blast of fiery pain.

"You don't have to do that, Jack!" the thickset man protested.

"Shut up! Shut up! We're doing this *my* way now! You had your chance and we almost messed up!"

"The boss wants him alive."

"Alive, sure! That don't say we can't make sure he's real quiet and polite for the trip back!"

"Jack!"

"If you don't like it, just shut your yap!" The skinny kid half turned to his companion and Holroyd, still flat on the ground.

Buchanan, already collapsed in a bent position, slid his hand under his pantleg and pulled the holdout gun from the top of his boot.

The skinny kid saw the movement and started to wheel back with frightening quickness. He wasn't fast enough. Buchanan's first shot hit him high in the chest somewhere and the second took the top of his head off. He was knocked over backwards.

Buchanan swung the gun toward the thicker man and fired a third time. The shot hit him high somewhere, tumbling him back a step to teeter for an instant and then plunge out of sight into the wash Buchanan had so recently vacated. There was a commotion of falling rock and dirt in the wash, brush being crushed, and then the skinny kid was flopping in death spasms beside Holroyd, who scrambled uncertainly to his feet.

"My God!" the deputy choked. "I never saw a man move that fast!"

"How bad is it?" Buchanan demanded.

"The shot went clean through my horse's neck, hit me here in the arm. The shock knocked me down. I don't think it's too bad."

"Find your gun on the ground, there." Buchanan turned and rushed to the edge of the

197

wash, peering over cautiously to see what had happened to the thickset man.

He didn't see anything, but from down the wash several feet away came the sound of somebody running through the brush, scattering rock and gravel.

"He's getting away," Holroyd grated, limping up to Buchanan's side. "Let's get after him!"

"You know how much chance we've got of catching him in this dark?" Buchanan panted.

As if to emphasize his question, there was the sudden explosion of hoofbeats downslope. The other gunman had reached his horse and was getting out of there.

"That was Slater," Holroyd said, gasping for air as he clutched his injured arm. He limped back to the dead man and turned him over with a push of his boot. "Hell, I forget this one's name. Just went to work for Pilgrim. Had a big rep."

"Well, he's got a dead rep now," Buchanan said. The shakes had started in his inevitable reaction to violence.

"They followed me and I didn't know it," Holroyd said between his teeth. "I was stupid."

"Sit down on this rock. Let me wrap something around that arm before you leak everything you've got left in you."

Holroyd obeyed. He seemed slightly dazed by his wound and the quickness of events. "Stupid. Just stupid. Didn't think it likely that they'd trail me. But I thought I was watching."

"It's damn dark," Buchanan told him, ripping a strip off his shirt and tying it around the black, bleeding holes in Holroyd's upper arm. "They were probably pretty good at it, too. Hey, that bullet

198

went clean through and didn't even get the bone. You might live."

Holroyd snorted something halfway between a cry and a laugh. "Thanks."

Buchanan sank back on his haunches, breathed deep, and discovered that he had lost his makings in the melee somewhere. "You were going to tell me about the hospital. About Margaret."

Holroyd looked at him with eyes that were dead in the starlight. "That's why I was late. I tried to track them. It was no use."

"What *happened?*" Buchanan bit off.

"They broke in the back. They took her."

"Took her?"

"Mrs. Ford. They took her out of St. Patrick and got away. She's gone."

NINETEEN

Buchanan sat down weakly on the ground. The feelings that swept over him were like an avalanche: shock, fear, anger, revulsion.

He said, "It's Pilgrim."

"Not for sure," Holroyd said.

"It's Pilgrim! He couldn't see her in the hospital anymore and he wants to get at me, so he had her kidnapped."

Squatting beside him, Holroyd muttered with concern. "Christ, man! You fixed my arm, and you're bleeding like a stuck pig!" He pressed a bandana to the bonfire gash on the side of Buchanan's face.

Buchanan ignored the pain. "I've got to go get her."

"I'll go," Holroyd argued. "You're hurt worse than I am. He'll be watching for you, be ready to kill you, and the law will be on his side. If she's there, I'll find her."

Buchanan pushed him away and staggered to his feet, some of his fear and hurt transforming itself into an implacable rage. "I'm going for her."

"I told you—"

"I can get across to the east to that next bunch of mountains under cover of dark tonight, then work my way south during the day, watching for posses, staying in the trees. By tomorrow dark I can be over the ridge yonder and down into his valley." Buchanan paused and looked at Holroyd, who seemed sharper than reality, etched in superblack contrast against the starlit sky. "You've got to tell me the terrain. The layout of his ranch. How the house lays. Everything."

"Goddammit!" Holroyd cried. "You're hurt, and you won't have a chance! Hell, this whole thing could be a trap just to get you to walk in there, and you're talking about doing just what Pilgrim expects!"

Buchanan picked the skinny youth's gun off the ground and stuck it in the back of his belt under his vest. He reloaded and replaced his holdout gun in his boot. Then he looked around, found his Colt, and holstered it. He felt light-headed, yet was preternaturally clear in his mind about what he had to do.

"You just can't do it," Holroyd told him, grasping him by the shoulder. "It's insane! You're walking into a trap!"

"He's got Margaret," Buchanan said. "I'm going."

She felt she would suffocate. Or be beaten to death by the tumbling she was taking in the back of the fast-moving carriage on a rough road.

Margaret had been fitfully sleeping when the sound of boots on the hollow wood floor aroused her. For a moment she had thought it must be Sister Immaculata, but the footsteps were too heavy and rough for it to be her. Then she had thought it must be Dr. Stone, but there were too many sounds. And then the door had flown open, and in the faint light from the street window she had seen the two men with cloths over their mouths.

She started to scream but they were faster. One grabbed her and put his hand over her mouth, choking off breath as well as sound. The other turned her arm behind her back, sending a wrenching agony through her shoulder, and when she opened her mouth against the other man's hand to cry out in pain, he stuffed a foul-smelling rag between her teeth, gagging her.

She might have fainted for a few seconds. When next she had been shocked fully conscious, they were carrying her somewhere. Ropes harshly bound her ankles and wrists, and all she could see were their arms and the blurry dark of the alley, and then a carriage. They had tossed her roughly into the back of the carriage and pulled a canvas fully over her.

"Go!" a man's voice had rasped, and the carriage had bolted into movement.

That had been long ago; indeed the swift, jarring ride seemed endless. Every jounce into a hole or over a bump was transmitted directly into her body, and the pain was considerable. At first she had felt sheer panic, sure the foul rag in her mouth would choke her to death. *It's not that bad, it's not that bad,* she had fought with her panic. *You can breathe through your nose, you're not dying.*

Now she was freezing, and cold night wind blew steadily under a corner of the canvas covering her. She smelled pine and water. They must be in the country somewhere. She fought her panic some more. She had to—if she stopped fighting for control even a moment, she felt she would go over

202

a precipice of insanity and never be able to return.

The carriage pace slowed and she sensed they were climbing a steep mountain grade. The chill deepened. She felt nauseated, and thus met a new source of terror: if she vomited, she would strangle on her own fluids.

She was disoriented, her thinking only intermittently clear. She fought that, struggled to stay in contact with the present.

Getting away from Pilgrim, seeing Jimmy again, being at the hospital had done that much for her already, she realized. She had begun to understand the damage her mind had sustained.

You can stay in control, she told herself.

She only half believed it, but she clung to sanity as best she could.

The endless ride went on. She lapsed into unconsciousness.

When she snapped back, the motion had stopped. She sensed by the stiff pain all over her body that hours had passed.

She heard voices. Men.

"It went according to plan?"

"Just right."

"She isn't hurt?"

"No. sir."

"No pursuit?"

"Nobody even seen us. We was gone before they knew what happened."

"Good. Bring her inside."

Lantern light flared in through the corner of the canvas and the carriage shook. Margaret clenched her eyes tightly shut, feigning unconsciousness. Hands grasped her, shoulders and legs, lifting her, carrying her. Through closed eyelids she detected the pink evidence of nearby lantern light, then darkness, then more subdued light. The air was warmer and the footsteps sounded hollowly on a wood floor. She was inside, then.

"Upstairs. The second door on the right."

She recognized the voice: Lucas Pilgrim. She almost gave into despair and panic, but fought. She was *not* helpless, she was not, she lectured herself. She was fully in contact with reality—hanging on somehow—and that was what they could not anticipate. She had a chance.

She had to believe she had a chance.

Her body was tilted dizzyingly as she was carried up a flight of stairs. Then footsteps rustled on carpet, a door creaked, and she was being carried into warmer air and stretched out on a soft surface—a bed.

The canvas was pulled off her and more light assailed her closed eyelids.

"She's unconscious! Are you sure she's all right?"

"She fainted, boss. That's all."

A second or two of silence, then, *"I'll have the housekeeper look in on her. Let's get out of here now before she wakes."*

Footsteps again, and the sound of a door closing gently but firmly.

The sound of a key turning in a heavy lock.

Guardedly, Margaret opened her eyes.

She lay on a big canopy bed, pale pink flowers in the ivory-colored material of the covers and the canopy. The bedroom was large, with high ceiling, dark blue carpet on the floor, a dresser and mirror, a closet, a window with pale chintz curtains. Everything looked fresh and expensive.

She was in Lucas Pilgrim's house, then.

She sat up on the edge of the bed. Dizziness flooded her, but she got her bearings and forced herself to her feet, then crept to the window.

Sharp disappointment washed through her. The window had shutters on the outside—strong oak shutters—and they were fully closed, evidently locked or nailed from the outside.

She moved around the room. *Jail,* she thought. *It's like a jail.* She felt claustrophobia stir, and she wanted to scream, wanted to let go and retreat into the confusion that had been her safe harbor all these months.

If you do that, you're lost.

She clung to sanity.

Returning to the bed, she sat on its edge and looked at the raw places on her wrists where the ropes had been cut. She didn't remember when that had been done. She wondered if she was as sane and in contact as she thought she was.

What was going to happen next?

She thought of Lucas Pilgrim, the size of him, the ugly brute force that radiated out of his body. She had sensed his desire for her. Thinking of that, she shuddered and felt the bile in her throat again.

Clenching her hands into fists, she struggled against panic.

As dawn neared, one of the original posses gave it up and their members straggled into Missoula, or to their homes. A new group was formed. Someone reported seeing the fugitive east of town, and someone else reported with equal certainty that he was west. A nervous sheepherder thought he saw something suspicious and shot twice, killing one of his own best ewe lambs. Men blundered around in the night, losing track of one another and secretly wishing (some of them) that they could call the whole thing off.

It was *cold* out here!

In the mountains well to the east of the search area, two men moved steadily toward higher ground, working farther east and then south. Riding their remaining horse double, they stayed in the trees and followed the deepest switchbacks for additional cover.

At dawn they holed up and slept for a while, and then pressed on again because they had a long way to go yet, to be ready by nightfall.

TWENTY

The day came brilliant with sunshine, a low northern wind making the air cool. Birds sang in the birch trees near the sprawling ranch house. Through a crack in the thick shutters that made her a prisoner, Margaret could see part of the side yard: a birch and a tamarack, one distant corner of a great white barn, a length of fencing, and, occasionally, a hired hand walking from the barn area to some other work station out of her vision. Distantly, men called to one another as they worked cattle.

The house was as silent as an enormous tomb.

Some two hours after sunup, the key turned in the lock on Margaret's door and a manservant, very old, opened the door for Mrs. Devine, the housekeeper, who then entered carrying a tray of breakfast and steaming tea. Margaret got the briefest glimpse of someone else on guard in the hall, a much younger man, roughly dressed, armed. The elderly manservant discreetly closed the door and went away.

Mrs. Devine carried the tray to the table beside Margaret's bed. She was a buxom woman, steel gray, in her fifties, with the determined cheerfulness of the well-paid servant. Last night she had bathed Margaret's face and wrists and ankles, pretended the bruises did not exist, refused to answer questions, and left after providing a tin cup of fresh milk.

"My, we're up early today," she said, uncovering the dishes on the tray. "You slept well?"

"When do I see Mr. Pilgrim?" Margaret demanded.

"I have no idea, my dear," Mrs. Devine said in the same lighthearted tone. "You like hot cereal, I hope?"

Margaret almost succumbed to the impulse to scream and kick her feet like a thwarted child. Instead, intent on being as unthreatening as possible, she sat on the edge of the bed and began her breakfast. The oat cereal was sweeter than she preferred, and the biscuits slightly burned, but the tea was something she needed, and brewed just right.

While Mrs. Devine moved aimlessly around the room, adjusting and dusting things that needed neither, Margaret ate everything up.

"I'm so pleased you're feeling so well!" Mrs. Devine told her. "Mr. Pilgrim said you were visiting us for a few days because you've been feeling so poorly."

Margaret remembered she was supposed to be crazy—as crazy as she had been before the shock of her abduction had somehow wrenched her into greater clarity than she had known for months.

She gave Mrs. Devine what she hoped was a confused look. "Can you tell me, please, how much it snowed last night?"

"Snowed? Why, my dear, it didn't snow at all! You're confused!"

"But I thought it always snowed on Christmas," Margaret murmured.

"On Chr—" Mrs. Devine stopped abruptly, frowning. "Oh. I see. Yes, dear. I think you may be just a little under the weather."

"Under the weather?" Margaret singsonged. "Oh, that's funny! And I just *asked* about the weather!"

Mrs. Devine, despite her bulk and obvious strength, looked uneasily toward the closed door. Margaret used the moment to slip the knife off her tray and into the bedclothes. Mrs. Devine turned back. "If you're finished, dear, we need to take a walk down the hall."

Margaret stood, curious. Mrs. Devine picked up the tray and scowled at it. "You've lost some of your silverware. Where could it have gone?" She looked around on the floor and then flipped the rumpled bed coverlets back, revealing the knife. "There it is," she smiled, and replaced it on the tray. "Come, dear. Follow me."

Margaret hid her disappointment and followed the big woman to the door. Mrs. Devine rapped once, sharply, and it opened from the other side. The manservant and the guard were both standing there. They got out of the way as Mrs. Devine put the tray on a chair in the hall and gestured for Margaret to follow her.

Margaret obeyed, conscious that the guard trailed discreetly behind.

The upstairs hallway of Lucas Pilgrim's house was as wide as the Ford cabin. Rich carpet and oil paintings provided color, luxury. The doors to the rooms along the long corridor were stout oak, uniformly closed to prying eyes. Margaret was led away from the near end, where the hall opened into a great white stairwell with a curving bannister and an enormous crystal chandelier, only partly visible. She was being taken in the opposite direction, deeper into the house.

Mrs. Devine finally stopped at a door like all the others. She took a key from her apron, unlocked the door, and motioned Margaret in. Margaret went in and caught her breath with surprise and pleasure.

It was another bedroom, much larger than hers, with windows thrown open to the sun and a cool, sweet breeze. The view was magnificent, stretching out over the Pilgrim land to distant, gleaming mountains. The walls of the room were stark white, the bed covers and draperies a lavish rose red. Every detail, from the delicate pottery basin and pitcher on the white dresser to the freshly cut wildflowers on the small, feminine desk in one corner, bespoke good taste and loving attention.

Mrs. Devine saw Margaret's reaction. "It was Mrs. Pilgrim's room. He loved her very much."

Margaret said nothing, shocked that this side of Lucas Pilgrim existed.

Mrs. Devine led her across the room to a wall of doors and flung them open to reveal a closet as large as another room. The closet was filled with row after row of dresses, shoes, hats, and other beautiful woman's garments.

"Mr. Pilgrim says you had no time to pack, and have no clothes. He wants you to select whatever you need or wish from his wife's things."

"Oh," Margaret murmured in dismay, "I couldn't do that!"

"Oh, but he wants you to, my dear."

Margaret hesitated, torn between delight with the wealth before her—more than she could ever have dreamed of—and fear of the hidden hook in this treasure. Why was she being treated like a queen when she had been so callously abducted? What lay behind these stratagems?

Somehow, such seeming kindness frightened her much more than other approaches might. What was he going to do to her?

Early in the afternoon, Sheriff J. D. Abercrombie, with four of his special temporary deputies from Missoula, rode onto Pilgrim property from the west, using Deadman Pass. He hadn't gone a mile over the invisible line denoting the edge of Pilgrim's domain when he saw the first rider high on a bluff to his south, watching him and his men. The lone rider turned in full view of the sheriff and his men far below and signalled to the east with something—probably a small mirror—that glinted blindingly in the clear mountain sun.

Abercrombie was impressed.

A little farther on, after passing a small herd of Pilgrim cattle along a fast-moving mountain stream, the sheriff and his men crossed the gouged-out road where wagons passed regularly on the way to Missoula, taking out felled trees from Pilgrim's logging operations. In this area, moving through rougher country where the sides of mountains stood almost vertical over impossibly deep ravines, Abercrombie spotted another watcher high up.

In another little while the sheriff's group passed close to a wooded hillside where Abercrombie could see in the far distance the wood structures and clutter of one of Pilgrim's many small mines. It was said Pilgrim regularly found enough silver to pay for the mining operations, and sometimes a little gold in addition. Nobody knew for sure, however. Pilgrim often set up a small digging op-

211

eration, worked it for a while, then closed it and tried somewhere else. Men whispered that some of the closed shafts had looked good—they had it from somebody else who had worked there, seen the vein. But nobody could testify first-hand on that, either.

Leaving the roughest country behind, Abercrombie and his men moved into the broad, open valley where Pilgrim was headquartered.

More than twenty miles it stretched from end to end, with the Blackfoot River cutting across its broadest girth and two smaller streams, the Big Fish and the Lady, making smaller, tree-lined excursions. Some parts of the valley had been clear to begin with, and other parts had been timbered, with the result that it sprawled, vast, emerald, open, fences crisscrossing at long intervals, trees forming breaks along the streams. Lazy clusters of brown dots were scattered over the entire area that was in view, signifying the bulk of Pilgrim's extensive herds. It was a beautiful, a magnificent, view. Anyone looking out over it would have known that the man who owned and ran all this was enormously rich and powerful.

Abercrombie, who had never had much and who knew he owed his job to Pilgrim, swallowed a clot in his throat and signalled his men to ride with him downslope. They headed directly toward the distant woods in the very center of the valley, out of which gleamed hints of the roofs of barns, storage buildings, bunkhouses, and the huge stone structure that Lucas Pilgrim called home.

It was past three o'clock when they rode up the long graveled road through the pine woods and reached the vast grassy area surrounding the house itself.

212

A rider cantered out from the barns downslope and met them. "If you'll come this way with me, you can rest the horses and wash up. Sheriff, Mr. Pilgrim will meet you in the house as soon as you've had a chance to clean up a little."

Abercrombie took the hint, scrubbing his face and hands at the wellhouse behind the visitors' tackroom, then putting on his other shirt in the part-timers' bunkhouse. Then Enderly, whose chill quality made the sheriff's skin crawl, escorted him up to the house.

Lucas Pilgrim met Abercrombie in his office, a large room, its walls covered with area maps and its air thick with the stench of cold cigars. Pilgrim was smoking another one and the light from windows overlooking his valley shone pink on his blunt, bald head as he paced the room.

"You made good time, my friend."

Abercrombie swallowed. "Came as quick as I got your message."

"You brought men." It wasn't a question but a statement. Pilgrim knew; he knew everything that happened around here.

"Four," Abercrombie told him.

"Good. I assume your posses haven't found our man?"

"Not when I left. We had reports, but—"

"Two of my men got a glimpse of him yesterday."

This was news. Abercrombie jerked. "Whereabouts?"

"That doesn't matter. The point is that Buchanan killed one of my men—a senseless, cold-blooded shooting from ambush—and my other man narrowly got away with a bullet in his shoulder. He got back here after dawn this morning.

213

He'll be all right, barring infection. As a matter of fact, he'll be on duty again tonight. But I'm convinced now, Sheriff, that this madman will stop at nothing to get me, and that's why I wanted you and some men here."

"You think he's the one that abducted the woman in town?" Abercrombie asked.

"Of course." Pilgrim stared at him with eyes like bullets. "Who else is there to suspect?"

The sheriff had a couple of thoughts on that, but he was not about to mention them. "Nobody, I guess. So you think this man is nuts enough to try to come *here?*"

"I'm convinced of it. That's why I want you here, with some men."

"Well, sir," Abercrombie said dubiously, "we'll do all we can. But I don't have enough to cover every angle—"

"I have plenty of men. Look here." Pilgrim walked to the wall map of the valley and surrounding country and pointed with a blunt finger. "I have men on watch here . . . and here . . . over on this side at three places . . . and down here by the river. In addition, along this ridge I have two men riding back and forth, and my cattle crews out through this section have been alerted. I'm deploying three other close-in scouts at this very hour. No, sheriff, when that fool tries to come through to carry out his vendetta against me personally, he'll be stopped."

Impressed, Abercrombie stared at the map. It looked like an ant couldn't get through Pilgrim's defenses. "Then why do you need—"

"Sheriff, he must have that poor woman hidden somewhere by now. My men will try to take him alive so we can force him to reveal where he has her hidden. We'll turn him over to you for that. But if they can't take him alive—if he has to be killed to stop him—I want you here to witness that we had no choice."

Abercrombie looked up from the map and met Pilgrim's eyes. He felt a distinct twinge. Looking into those icy eyes was like looking into hell. The sheriff knew right then that his escaped prisoner, Buchanan, had no chance at all if he tried to come here.

In the mountains overlooking Lucas Pilgrim's kingdom from the north, Buchanan lowered Pat Holroyd's small brass spyglass from his eye and rested his vision for a moment. He lay flat on his belly on a bare granite outcropping that afforded a vast, panoramic view.

Hidden behind him in the deep fern cover of the woods, Holroyd continued his exhausted sleep. To Buchanan's front, two miles downslope and three thousand feet below, Pilgrim's valley sprawled under a pale bluish haze. Far off to the left gleamed the snowclad Garnet range, and closer to the right, the Sapphires. The grandeur of the scene got through to Buchanan for a few seconds, and he let his vision focus on distance. But then he forced himself to raise the spyglass again and resume his observation.

About an hour passed. His cracked ribs throbbed and so did his head. The side of his skull felt like somebody had tried to drive an auger through it. He was hungry and sour in the gut. But he tried to ignore those things and see every move far below.

After a while there was vague sound behind

him, Holroyd awakening, relieving himself, coming through the undergrowth to crawl up on the flat rock overhang and join him.

Buchanan glanced keenly at him, seeing how pale he was. "You all right?"

"Couldn't be better," Holroyd said with a thin smile. "What do you make out down there?"

Buchanan pointed out across the blue haze. "He's got men stationed all around the home area. Four, right now, just riding parts of a big circle about a mile out. There's a man on top of the barn with a glass like yours; you can just make him out because he sticks up. It looks like the drovers with the cattle—over to the east and down there to the south—are keeping the herds bunched, looking around for us as much as doing anything with the cows. I've spotted three other men riding around farther out: one down in the river bottom, one in that clump of trees there off to the west of the knob, and a third along the creek bottom off over there."

"Shit," Holroyd said. "If you can see that many, there are more."

Buchanan nodded agreement. "Also, it looked like Abercrombie and three or four cronies rode in a couple of hours ago."

Holroyd groaned. "What do *they* want?"

"My rear end, I imagine," Buchanan told him mildly.

"You seem awfully damned calm, all of a sudden, for a man that's looking down at an army laid out against him!"

"I feel better," Buchanan admitted.

"Why?"

"Because in about four hours it's going to be dark. And then we move."

216

"He *knows* you'll come. He's got a practically impenetrable defense perimeter set up down there! Our chances of getting through to the house—"

"Pat. Do you want to forget it?"

"No!"

"I can go alone."

"No, goddammit! I'm going! I just don't understand why you're so cheerful, seeing how the trap is laid out."

"We can get through."

"And even if we do? What then?"

"We take Margaret out of there."

"And Pilgrim?"

Buchanan started to speak, then seemed to think better of it. "I'm going to get an hour's sleep if I can. Do you feel good enough to keep watch out here?"

For answer, Holroyd took the spyglass from him.

Buchanan nodded and crawled back off the flat rock outcropping without another word. There was some minor commotion in the ferns as he vanished into the trees, then silence.

Holroyd scanned the valley below. He hurt. His head buzzed and he thought the chilled sensations in his body meant the start of fever from his gunshot wound. He didn't feel good about Buchanan's plan. But he couldn't come up with anything better. Sometimes a man had to handle things this way, or not at all.

He knew why Buchanan hadn't answered when asked about Pilgrim, and the reason defined his dilemma as a lawman.

If they were detected trying to reach the house through all Pilgrim's guards, they were as good as dead, in all likelihood. But if they made it, then

Pilgrim was almost certainly the dead one. There was no way this could turn out very good.

But that, Holroyd told himself, was not the kind of thinking that made a man's hungry gut stop hurting. They had no choice. They were going. Now they simply had to find the best route down there, the one that afforded them the best chance of survival.

So thinking, he raised his spyglass to his eye and started scanning.

Trembling but hanging onto her sanity, Margaret walked into the upstairs sitting room where Mrs. Devine had just directed her. The housekeeper herself had turned discreetly away to wait outside in the hallway.

It was another big room, windows festooned with dark red draperies, bare wood floor gleaming, dark mahogany furniture scattered along the walls, a fireplace burning cheerily against the gathering night.

Lucas Pilgrim turned from the twilit windows. Wearing a black suit, white shirt, and string tie, the glitter of diamonds in his cuffs, he looked her up and down with an intensity that sent panic coursing through her.

"My dear Margaret! You are magnificent!"

Margaret froze, watching him advance across the room, hands reaching toward her. She had had to wear some of the clothing from his dead wife's wardrobe, and had chosen the simplest pale lavender dress and most basic shoes she could find. But with her hair tied atop her head, her face scrubbed pink in the bath, her eyes wide with apprehension, she had known, as she looked at herself in the full-length mirror a little while ago, that she had failed if it had been her intent to look ugly. The dress was simple, high-necked, long-sleeved, almost without ornament. But it fit her perfectly, nipping in at her tiny waist, defining her bust and hips. She realized she looked lovely, wished she didn't, had no control.

Now, as Pilgrim took her hands in his great paws, drinking her in with his eyes, she realized that a sane man would never have kept his dead wife's wardrobe intact, her room like a shrine, or have wanted another woman to dress in these clothes for him unless his intentions were the worst imaginable.

"That was always one of my favorite dresses," he told her, still grasping her hands.

Margaret pulled away. "Why did you have me kidnapped? What kind of a man are you? How *dare* you just have me stolen away, brought here, held prisoner?"

"Margaret, Margaret," Pilgrim sighed, holding her at arms' length as if she were a child. "It was for your own good. I had no choice."

Her outraged anger was so great that she forgot her plan to pretend she had again lost her mind. "For my own good?" she spat. "Was it for my own good that you practically held me prisoner, a waitress for money that would get me free, but which never came?"

"I was doing what I considered best for you, Margaret—"

"Was it for my own good that you forced your way into the hospital with that paper I'll *never* sign?"

"Oh, but you will sign it, my dear," Pilgrim told her.

"No!"

"There are things you don't know."

"You killed my husband!"

"No. That was . . . an unfortunate accident."

He seemed so monolithically *sure of himself*. For a split second she again doubted her own sanity. She struggled. "Joe had a map. Whatever was there was stolen when he was murdered."

"Not exactly," Pilgrim told her.

The partial admission shook her further. "I—what?"

"There was a map," Pilgrim said. "It did lead to something. That something later came into my hands. Ever since then, I have been trying to make sure that no one else is hurt because of it, that what is rightfully yours is protected."

"You're a liar! You don't make sense!"

Pilgrim grasped her wrist and gently but firmly propelled her across the room. For the first time she saw that there was an object on the floor near the far wall, near the gaping door of a great steel safe.

The object on the floor was a strongbox, perhaps two feet long, half that size in its other dimensions. It was old, crusted by rust on the edges and around the broken hasp on its closed lid.

"This was what your husband found before he died," Pilgrim told her. "This is *yours*. Everything I've done has been designed to keep this secret, protect you from the harm that would surely come to you if people knew you had it."

"But you've kept it," Margaret flung back. "How can it be mine when you've had it?"

"Because it came from around here somewhere. I've been working to tie up all the surrounding land—including yours—so we can find where this

220

came from . . . you and I . . . and go on to-gether."

She reeled. *"Together? I can't believe—"*

With the pointed toe of his black leather boot, Pilgrim tipped the lid of the box open.

The evening light flowing through the windows fell on the box's contents, which seemed to come afire.

Margaret stared, her breath gone. The box was nearly filled with beautiful rocks, gemstones of some kind. Some were pale yellow, some almost transparent, some milky-colored and embedded in dirt or rock. But the majority were blue, all shades of blue from the color of a thinly clouded sky to to the most intense azure. Some were dull, many broken, brilliant where they had cracked along crystal faults. It was these brilliant edges that threw the lowering sun into her eyes with such intensity.

"Sapphires," Pilgrim said. "Some of the finest sapphires ever found in any of these mountains."

"Where did they come from?" Margaret gasped.

"They belonged to an old mountain man—"

"Eb Craddock!"

"Yes. He hid them and made a map. Evidently he gave the map to your husband before he died and your husband followed it and found this box. Then he was killed by thieves—"

"Your men!"

Pilgrim inclined his head with every semblance of sadness. "Two of my men. Yes. They were apprehended by me, punished." He gave her a look of blazing intensity. "Neither of them is alive now."

Inwardly Margaret reeled. This was too much information to take in at once. She no longer

221

knew what to believe. "But if they were Joe's, mine—"

"Margaret! These were dug somewhere near your property! If word had gotten out, with so much land uncontrolled, you would have been overrun, almost certainly claim-jumped—killed. Thus, when I learned of your mental state, I judged it best to hide you for a while, try to find the mother lode, buy up the land—"

"To buy my land! Yes! To steal everything!"

"I intend no such thing, Margaret. Not now. Because now you're going to sign the deed over to me, and then you shall have this chest in payment. You can go away, never see this land or any of us again."

"I don't believe you when you say your men killed Joe without your knowledge," she said, and now she had begun to weep. "From the beginning your only plan has been to get everything, to leave the rest of us with nothing."

"Did you know," Pilgrim shot back, "that Jim Buchanan has been charged with murder?"

"What?"

"One of my men was killed. I have a witness who says Buchanan did it in cold blood. He was jailed, but broke out. He is being hunted like a dog at this hour."

It was a savage blow, one that made her feel her last defenses begin to shred. "No. No."

"He's trying to come here," Pilgrim went on remorselessly. "He knows you're here. He'll be a heroic fool and come."

"You'd better hope he doesn't. Because if he does—"

"When he does, Margaret, he'll find that everything is not as it appears to be. And then he'll die—very painfully and meaninglessly—unless you have signed this paper."

"Are you saying he'll be spared if I sign?"

"If you sign, you will be wealthy. I will have no more quarrel with Buchanan. The law will be allowed to take its course. With luck, you can contact him, use your wealth to get him out of here. You can live happily ever after."

She could hardly believe such cruelty. Surely it was all a trick. "I'll never sign. And *then* what happens to all your plans?"

"He dies. And as for you, if I can't have the land, Margaret, if I can't have your cooperation, then I'll have another prize, even if it's a bitter one."

She stared at him. His eyes had changed, seemed to glow with the lust suddenly naked in them. Involuntarily she took a step back.

Pilgrim moved faster. He caught her wrist again, twisted her sharply so that she was spun around—into his arms. He crushed her against him. By sheer strength tilted her head back. His mouth descended and found hers.

Wanting to scream in revulsion, but unable to do even that, Margaret tried to fight him. He held her tighter. She could feel his hardness against her, pressing tighter. His tongue burst through her lips, pried her teeth apart, probed. The foul taste and odor of his cigars filled her mouth. She was helpless. She felt her fragile hold on sanity and reality tear into a thousand pieces, and experience became a jumbled confusion of terror, pain, despair.

TWENTY-ONE

Night came, and with it a clear, starry night and the sliver of a rising moon. The ground quickly gave off its heat and in the dark it was cold, the kind of cold that sinks quickly to the bone.

Buchanan and Holroyd had moved cautiously down the mountainside in the early evening, leading their horse, and by the time full darkness was at hand, they were ready to move out.

The clarity of the night was anything but a help. As the two men moved out of the brush cover at the foot of a hill littered with fallen rock, the grassy valley was fully visible all around them, and the starlight so bright that Buchanan could actually see faint shadows.

He told himself they could turn the brilliance of the night to their advantage.

As planned, Holroyd swung into the saddle. Buchanan trotted across the meadow to the darker line which marked willows and tamaracks following the path of a tiny stream. Staying in the cover of the trees, he moved eastward on foot, generally in the direction of the distant ranch complex, paralleling the route taken by Holroyd, who rode along in full view at a casual pace.

They knew where they were likely to encounter the first outrider, and it took nearly an hour to

224

get to that point. Holroyd twice paused in full view in the starlight to build a cigarette and light it, the flare of his match a bright red spot in the silvery night. It was important for him to look casual and unhidden—a friend—and the pauses let Buchanan, working hard on foot in the brush, to catch up.

The first outrider was just where they had marked him earlier in the day, and right on time.

The creek curved slightly north at this point. Holroyd, riding in the open to Buchanan's left, was about twenty feet away. The ground sloped down into the creek here, blocking any view of them from the distant ranch house, putting them in a kind of natural halfmoon depression marked by bare, eroded dirt and a few boulders uncovered by the erosion.

The outrider came into view from Buchanan's right, beyond the curve in the stream. The rider reined up. His voice came clear, tense: *"Who's that there?"*

"Me," Holroyd replied at once, his voice ringing confidently. "They said for me to come relieve you."

The outrider walked his horse closer to Holroyd, who had reined up to stand in place. *"Thought I was on till midnight."*

"Change of plans," Holroyd said easily.

The outrider moved past Buchanan's hiding position and got within a few paces of Holroyd, who remained sitting still. The rider's voice suddenly changed, tension reappearing.

"Say, do I know you? Who the hell are you, anyway?"

By the time the words were out, Buchanan was in motion, running behind him. His length of

225

pine was four feet long, and heavy with resin.

"Well, you know," Holroyd was saying, "I haven't been on the payroll very long, and—"

The outrider heard Buchanan and started to turn. Buchanan, rushing within reach, swung the pine branch. The rider moved violently and the branch missed.

At the same moment, Holroyd jerked his horse into motion, slamming into the other rider's mount. The outrider tried to react, but wasn't fast enough. Holroyd's good arm swung and something made a clunking sound as the outrider's hat fell off and he tumbled slowly out of the saddle.

Buchanan caught his horse's reins in time and calmed the animal. Holroyd was out of his saddle in a second and bent to examine the outrider, unconscious on the ground.

"That was close," Buchanan muttered.

"Help," Holroyd suggested.

The two of them dragged the unconscious man into the high brush. Holroyd put a wad of cloth in his mouth and tied it in place while Buchanan bound his wrists and ankles. The outrider would be missed, but probably not until his relief man came at midnight.

Buchanan and Holroyd hurried back to the horses. Buchanan took the outrider's mount, a quiet, easily handled gray. They glanced at each other, hope rising. They had made it through the first phase. Without a word they turned their mounts and rode slowly out of the earthen depression and onto higher ground. As they had planned, Holroyd turned south and Buchanan north.

Helen Devine was fifty-five years old, and she

had never worked for an employer she could not admire and even, in her way, consider family.

She had worked for Lucas Pilgrim as house-keeper and home manager since his marriage twenty years ago. She was a woman of stern morality and the highest principles.

She had always known that Lucas Pilgrim had the same qualities.

He was, after all, rich and powerful. Growing up as she had in a poverty-stricken Irish ghetto of Chicago, Helen Devine had been taught from an early age that, though having money did not necessarily make a person morally admirable, there were many fine people in the world whose courage, intelligence, and hard work had led God to give them extra blessings, gifts they sometimes shared with less fortunate good people by employing them, making them part of their extended family.

Helen's parents had been servants, and their parents before them. They were good servants, good people, and turned in an honest day's work, respected their employers, could be trusted never to steal, betray a confidence, or so much as sulk.

Workers who were trash did those things.

Helen had married young and moved west, first to the Dakotas. Her husband died there in an attack by Sioux. Helen stayed for a while, then later moved west with a family named Kincade who paid her poorly but needed her a lot. When she met Lucas Pilgrim, he was soon to be married. He offered her four times her salary with the Kincades. She liked him—he was handsome in those days, lusty, reeking of power and wealth, all the things she had learned to respect—and she liked his bride, too.

The new Mrs. Pilgrim had always been wealthy, and knew how to direct servants while herself being ornamental and charming.

Mrs. Devine moved in, ran the household, was happy. She asked no questions about things that were none of her business.

When Mrs. Pilgrim died so unexpectedly, Mrs. Devine stayed on and became the virtual dictator of the Pilgrim household, making all decisions, hiring and firing other help, planning purchases and menus, so that Mr. Pilgrim never had to worry about any of that. To him she was a quiet, smiling ally. To the staff she was a terror; to the outside world, a stone wall.

Pilgrim paid her well. She could not have been happier in her role.

She believed he was strong, moral, kind, generous.

She wouldn't have worked for him if she thought otherwise.

But from the moment Lucas Pilgrim brought Margaret Ford into the house, Mrs. Devine sensed that something was very wrong indeed.

The girl was not well. Clearly, the way she was kept locked in her room, she was not entirely a willing guest. She had frightened Mrs. Devine when she had tried so awkwardly to steal a knife off the breakfast tray.

Mrs. Devine didn't like it, detected the sickly odor of something secret and unnatural and wrong when Pilgrim instructed her that Margaret was to use the dead Mrs. Pilgrim's wardrobe. It was *sick* to put another woman, especially a young and pretty one, in Mrs. Pilgrim's clothes. It was as if he were trying to bring her back in the form of this poor child.

For all of that, Mrs. Devine might have kept her place and looked the other way through practically anything.

Anything but taking the young woman, who looked eerily like the dead Mrs. Pilgrim in her dress, to Pilgrim's upstairs office, only to be summoned back a little later to find the child virtually *destroyed*.

Mrs. Devine felt deeply uneasy, as if she were doing something evil, when she took the younger woman down the hallway, into the room where Mr. Pilgrim waited. But she did it because she had always followed orders, secure in the belief that her employer was a good and benevolent man.

As she waited in the hall for the interview to be over, she was aware of her worry and tension.

Then she heard the voices raised beyond the closed door. She heard the sound of scuffling. She exchanged glances with the man standing nearby, and saw his eyes go opaque and turn away.

What was happening?

A few moments passed.

Then came the sound of a stifled scream.

It lanced into Mrs. Devine's heart. She had never heard a sound quite like that scream — muffled, cut short, broken, filled with unutterable despair.

The office door was flung open. Pilgrim, face brick-colored with ugly emotion and his clothes rumpled, had Margaret in the crook of his arm like a rag doll. The girl was totally changed.

Her first glance at Margaret was the most profound and awful shock Mrs. Devine had ever sustained.

Margaret was the color of old sheets. Her hair

had come down on one side. Her dress was torn partly off one shoulder. Her eyes were filled with sheer terror and disorientation. She looked—mad.

"Mrs. Ford has become ill," Pilgrim said brusquely. "Take her back to her room."

"What happened to her?" Mrs. Devine blurted.

"Goddamn you, woman! Remember your place here and do as you're told!" Pilgrim thrust Margaret forward and she would have tumbled to the carpet if Mrs. Devine hadn't been quick. As Mrs. Devine caught Margaret's limp weight, Pilgrim slammed the office door in her face.

Shocked to her core, Mrs. Devine snapped at the man standing there, "Help me!"

He obeyed. Together they carried Margaret back to her room. They stretched her out on the bed. He backed out quickly, the door closing softly behind him.

Mrs. Devine looked down at Margaret and tried to digest what had happened.

Margaret's eyes were dazed, her pupils pinpoints that focused on nothing. Her pallor was terrible to see, her mouth twisted, bruised. Dark marks of fingers that had clutched deeply were already forming on her bare shoulder.

"Child! What *is* it?"

"Oh, no," Margaret whimpered. "Oh, no, oh, no. I can't allow it. I'll never do that. Joe . . . *Joe!*"

Mrs. Devine clutched the girl to her, rocking her like a child. "It's all right," she crooned. "It's all right. You're safe."

"You killed him," Margaret whispered frantically. "You stole everything. Jimmy. Jimmy. He just wanted to help me. No. No. I can't allow that. I'll die. You'll never do it to me. Get your hands away from me. Get your mouth away from me. Stop. Stop."

The words were incoherent. The girl was hysterical. But the meaning behind her words hit Mrs. Devine with the force of a thunderbolt.

She rocked Margaret, crooning meaningless words of her own. Her mind raced as she did so, the shocking truth coming home. The child had walked into that room beautiful, young, vibrantly alive. She had come out only a few minutes later, shattered.

The torn dress, the bruised mouth and shoulder, told starkly what had happened to destroy her.

Mrs. Devine kept rocking Margaret in her arms, kept murmuring meaningless words, silly sounds, the kind one would croon to a frightened infant. After a while Margaret seemed to calm, staring blankly into space. Mrs. Devine slowly reclined her to the bed.

She had no idea what to do next.

The dress, she thought suddenly, staring at the torn fabric. The dress had to be repaired.

She hurried out of the bedroom, went downstairs, found the cook still in the kitchen, and got a glass of milk to take upstairs. On the way back with the milk, she stopped in her own room and got the sewing basket. She carried both past the guard and into Margaret's room again.

Margaret was sitting on the side of the bed, staring fixedly. Her eyes turned to Mrs. Devine as she entered.

"You're safe, child. I'll see to that."

"Where is Sister?" Margaret asked in the soft, bewildered tone of a little girl.

"Sister will be here."

"When? When?"

"Soon. Here. Drink this milk. It will calm you."

"I have to find my husband," Margaret said. "I have to cook for him. But I'm staying with Sister right now." She looked around. "Why is it dark? Isn't this Sunday morning?"

Mrs. Devine helped her drink the milk. She seemed more soothed after that. Mrs. Devine helped her out of the torn dress and into another, a plain white gown suitable for moving around the room, or for sleeping.

"I'll be back later, child."

"Where is Sister? I'm supposed to see Sister."

"Try to sleep. I'll look in on you later."

"Yes." Margaret stretched out on the bed and stared at the ceiling with wide, haunted eyes.

Mrs. Devine went to the door. The sewing basket was on the table there. She left it, along with the torn dress.

There would be many times later when she tried to remember exactly what she thought at that moment. She would never be sure if she had been thinking at all, or if her unconscious mind had taken over, guiding her actions with its wisdom.

However it happened, and why, Mrs. Devine left the sewing basket there, and left the room.

On top of the needles and thread and patchwork in the sewing basket, a pair of pointed scissors glittered.

Pilgrim caught her in the hallway before she reached her room. He had changed his shirt and coat, and seemed calmly in control again . . . the great man she had always admired and loved.

"Is she resting, Mrs. Devine?"

"Yes, sir."

"Good." Pilgrim patted her on the shoulder.

232

"She's very ill, I'm afraid. But with good care she will heal, I'm sure."

"Yes, sir."

Pilgrim did not notice her agitation. "I expect guests tonight, Mrs. Devine, but it's a business transaction that needn't affect you. Please go to your room and remain there until morning. All right?"

"Yes, sir," Mrs. Devine said for the third time. And obeyed him.

About forty minutes after separating from Pat Holroyd, Buchanan swung down off his horse in the shadows of a tiny grove of birch trees and left him tied there. He proceeded on foot, moving in a crouched position and stopping often to bend even deeper and freeze, trying to look to a roving eye like the lumpy shadow of a boulder.

Moving in this way, he covered several hundred yards, finally reaching the back wire fencing behind the corral and the barns just beyond. Ahead of him, on both sides of the corral, he could make out the shadows of men walking back and forth much like military sentries on duty. If he moved from this hiding place, they would see him at once.

He waited.

In a little while there was a distant commotion—men's voices raised well on the far side of the ranch house complex. The men close by stopped walking and called sharply to one another. There was more distant shouting and then a single gunshot.

Christ. Buchanan thought. *That's not in the script!*

233

The men walking a beat around the corral area yelled to people nearer the ranch house.

A voice called back shrilly, *"They got 'em over yonder! C'mon!"*

The guards on Buchanan's side of the complex appeared out of the shadows, running away from him and toward the voice.

Buchanan rose immediately, slid under the bottom fence wire, and trotted across the corral. The horses took alarm at his sudden appearance, and moved around in whirling confusion. Choking on their dust, he ran into the back doorway of the main barn.

The barn was vast and quiet. He crossed it to the far side, where pale night light shone through the double doors. Beyond the doors was a small garden plot, also fenced, and beyond that, a wellhouse and the vast blackness of the shade of the ranch house itself, which loomed like a monster against the starlit sky.

The sound of excited voices was louder on the far side, and glints of lantern light winked and flashed through the trees. Knowing how little time he had, Buchanan went over the garden fence and moved up the rows of vegetables, reaching the fence on the other side. Without hesitation he clambered over that, too, and ran for the corner of the wellhouse.

So far, so good. Pausing to get his breath, he peered around the corner of the building. He could see past the end of the ranch house from here, and clearly saw the dancing lanterns and a dozen or so men pushing their way up the slope. There was a lot of excited yelling, but then suddenly it fell off sharply.

"We got one of 'em!" somebody shouted.

A fainter voice from the front of the house called something in response.

"No, sir! It's the other 'un! No! He ain't hurt!"

Pat Holroyd had done his part, and done it well, Buchanan thought with intense relief.

Now it was up to him.

He circled around the far side of the wellhouse. Except for a shaggy grape arbor, there was nothing now between him and the back of the house. He moved out of hiding and crossed the few yards, passing the arbor, and climbed the back porch steps.

The back porch was enclosed in latticework. Under its roof everything was pitch black. Buchanan felt his way across the board flooring until his hands encountered the rock wall of the house itself. Then he probed along to his right until his hands encountered the back door molding.

There was a screen. He swung it open. The latchstring was inside, but he poked his index finger in through the hole and caught it, withdrawing it. He tugged it, then, and the latch was raised and the door swung partly open.

Thinking it was almost too easy, he slipped inside.

He was in a back storage room with a door opening into a part of the kitchen. The kitchen was dim and deserted, but from deeper inside the house he could hear men's voices:

"No, no, tell Sheriff Abercrombie to stay on watch out there! We don't have the other one yet!"

"Do we take this 'un out there?"

"No, leave him here. The rest of you get back on watch. Enderly, Murnan, Baxter, stay. I want to talk to you."

235

Buchanan moved across the storage room into the kitchen. Gun in hand, he entered a narrow back hall. Pilgrim still had three of his men with him, and that made it more complicated than he had hoped. But everything so far had gone well. And he had the advantage of surprise.

He crept along the hallway in the dark, moving toward the sound of voices. Ahead he saw the thin yellow bead of light that marked a closed door. There was another alcove of some sort to the left of the closed door, and he started to slip into that, taking a minute to plan his next move.

As he slid into the black alcove, something moved.

He simply had no time to react.

A paralyzing blow exploded on the back of his skull and he saw brilliant colors and then nothing at all.

TWENTY-TWO

Margaret had fallen into a dazed, fitful sleep as night fell. This had happened often since the first shock of her husband's murder and her grisly discovery of his body. Sleep was an automatic temporary escape from reality, a defense that her mind gave her without conscious volition.

The sounds of a distant gunshot and men's voices roused her.

Sitting up on the bed, she instantly remembered Lucas Pilgrim's harsh embrace and his mouth violating hers. Her mind almost flicked back into another kind of escape—disconnection from reality—but she caught herself just in time. *I will not go crazy!* she thought with fierce resolve, and somehow it worked.

Feeling feverish and unnaturally clearheaded, she left the bed and went to the shuttered window. Only blackness met her eyes. A moment of vertigo almost dropped her to her knees. She clung to the draperies and regained her balance.

The door of her room opened quietly. Hearing the sound, she turned and saw Mrs. Devine slip inside, closing the door quickly behind her. The older woman's icy composure was gone; she looked flushed, nervous, vulnerable.

She remained near the door, beside the table that held the sewing basket. Her eyes seemed to burn into Margaret.

237

"You're better?" Mrs. Devine whispered.

"I—yes," Margaret said.

"I don't know what's going on, child. There are men downstairs—outside. You heard the shot?"

"Yes. I'm frightened."

Mrs. Devine looked down in what could only be read as despair. "I have no power. I thought I was a *partner* here, a help. I've been told nothing. But I know that the things being done to you are wrong."

"He wants my land," Margaret told her in a rush. "He tried to make love to me—"

The housekeeper silenced her with a savage, slashing gesture of her bony hand. "I would help if I could. If a chance comes, I'll do anything I can to get you out of here. You are a captive? Being held against your will?"

"Yes."

"Dear God," Mrs. Devine breathed. She paused, then looked down at the sewing basket. She returned her gaze to Margaret in what was obviously a look heavy with meaning.

Then, without another word, she turned the knob in the door, pulled it open a scant few inches, and slipped out as quietly as she had come.

Puzzled, Margaret tried to understand the meaning of her visit as well as her words and expression. She sensed that she had an ally now, but didn't see how the older woman could help her.

Except that she had looked twice, meaningfully, at the sewing basket, which Margaret hadn't previously noticed.

Margaret crossed the room and looked at it now.

Saw the five-inch metal scissors, gleaming with

238

nickel plating, sharp-tipped, with strong black metal loop handles.

I could never do that.

Could I?

She remembered Pilgrim's fetid mouth violating hers.

She picked up the scissors and slipped them into the waist-band of her dress. The scissors felt hard against her body, but she looked into the mirror and saw that they were invisible.

Despite the crushing blow, Buchanan did not wholly lose consciousness for more than a few seconds. He was blurrily aware of someone calling out hoarsely, light flooding the floor where he lay in his own blood, hands grabbing him and dragging him into brilliant light, dumping him painfully on the floor again.

"Is he dead?" Pilgrim's voice.

"No. Just out."

"Look in his boot. He carries a holdout gun."

Reality went away for an instant and came back as someone pulled the little holdout gun from his boot. He was lying on his back on the bare wood floor, and the revolver he had taken from the dead kid in the mountains—the one he had stuck into his belt in back, under his vest—dug painfully into his spine.

"Henry. Go get Mrs. Ford."

Buchanan opened his eyes to slits. Painfully bright light flooded in. He saw Henry Slater, the one-eyed gunman he had met before, walk to the door. Slater looked pale and his left arm was in a sling. From the skirmish in the mountains where the other kid had died?

There was no time to ponder that. The one-eyed man left the room. Buchanan took in the rest of the room in one glance.

It was a drawing room, an overstuffed dark couch and chairs along two walls, a mahogany table holding a tall brass lamp with fringed shade, the door Slater had just exited through, a door that must lead outside at the other end. The windows were black with night, but distant lantern light sent glimmers across them in a random pattern.

Lucas Pilgrim stood near the windows, one hand holding a small pistol, the other a lit cigar. He was dressed in black, his bald dome gleaming in the light of the candle-bearing crystal chandelier. Across the room from him, two other men flanked Pat Holroyd, half supporting him between them. Holroyd was mud-splattered, and blood trickled down the side of his face from a wound in his hairline somewhere. One of the men supporting him was named Enderly—Buchanan remembered that, because the gunman's chill demeanor had impressed him before. He didn't know the other man.

Standing behind the couch to his right were two more hard cases, heavily armed, looking like they were capable of anything. He didn't recognize them.

One of them caught Buchanan's slit-eyed surveillance. "He's awake."

"Mr. Buchanan," Pilgrim said. "How nice of you to make this so easy for us."

Buchanan sat up and was rewarded with a kick in the side that knocked him over again in a cloud of pain.

"That will do, Lenny," Pilgrim said sharply.

Then, to Buchanan: "You must understand, sir, that any sudden movement may be taken as hostile, under the circumstances. You may sit up, but do so slowly."

Buchanan started getting his breath again and sat up on the floor.

Pilgrim puffed his cigar, slipped his little pistol into his coat pocket, and looked at Holroyd with a sad smile. "Pat, I'm surprised at you. I really am. You're supposed to uphold the law!"

"Your kind of law?" Holroyd asked bitterly.

"You never had a chance against me. Either of you."

"We came within an inch of making our plan work," Holroyd said.

Pilgrim chuckled and his men grinned. "Gentlemen, gentlemen! You still don't see? Do you imagine you would have gotten anywhere near the house if we hadn't made it easy for you?"

Holroyd looked stunned. He gave Buchanan a questioning look.

Pilgrim was enjoying himself. "When you ambushed my outrider, we had two other men close by observing you. You wouldn't have had to split up and take so long creeping up on the house, you know. All my men had instructions to be stupid, and let you get by them. And as for your idea of creating a disturbance on one side, while Mr. Buchanan, here, crept up from the opposite direction—well, gentlemen, what kind of fools do you think we are?"

Buchanan wiped blood from his mouth on his shirt sleeve. "You *let* us get this far?"

"Of course."

"Why?"

The inside door opened. Buchanan rocked back

with the impact of seeing Margaret come through the doorway. Henry Slater was right behind her, firmly holding her left arm behind her back in a painful vise.

Margaret's frightened eyes swept the room and found Buchanan. "Jimmy!" she moaned.

"Good, good," Pilgrim said. "Bring her here, Henry. That's it." He took Margaret's slender arm and held her beside him, helpless because any struggle she made would result in twisting her arm upward. Pilgrim could dislocate her shoulder if he wished, and he seemed to know this and take added pleasure from the knowledge.

"All right," the giant man said agreeably. He put his cigar in an ashtray and took out the small pistol again. "Lenny, Bax, Murnan, you can leave us alone. Please wait out on the front porch. Let no one else in."

The three men filed out of the room, briefly opening the front door to chill night air that gusted across the floor and over Buchanan. Their departure left Pat Holroyd standing unaided against the far wall, the impassive Enderly and Slater standing close to him, alert for anything. On the other side of the parlor, Pilgrim held Margaret close to his side.

"Now, then," he said pleasantly. "I believe it's time for business."

"Go straight to hell," Buchanan blurted.

Pilgrim's grin split his face. "Bless your heart, Mr. Buchanan! You don't seem to realize that I hold all the cards now. You'll play the hand I've given you, or none at all."

Margaret struggled weakly. "Why can't you leave us alone?"

Pilgrim raised her captive arm slightly, making

242

her go pale with pain. "Allow me to explain the situation, lady and gentlemen. And then we shall see what we shall see."

Tears slipped down Margaret's cheeks. Buchanan was so filled with fury he didn't trust himself to speak. Holroyd, also mute, stared with red-rimmed eyes that would have killed if they could.

Pilgrim's voice dripped with the kind of smug satisfaction that only comes when a man is sure he's already won. "Mr. Buchanan, you stand charged with murder, a charge you can never hope to be acquitted of as long as my man stands as witness against you. You stand doubly convicted by your jailbreak. Mr. Holroyd, you have aided an escaped killer and will not only lose your badge, but will also face a long prison term if charges are brought against you."

The hulking man paused to let that sink in, then went on, "Sheriff Abercrombie and some of his special deputies are outside, helping stand watch, as per my instructions. All I have to do is call them in and turn the both of you over to them, and your lives are finished."

"Get to the point, you bastard," Buchanan grated.

"The point to be made is not yours, Mr. Buchanan, but Mrs. Ford's." Pilgrim turned Margaret around with a rough movement, making her face him, pressed against the front of his massive body. "Margaret. None of this has to be. You can be reasonable. You can sign the deed, let me have the land, free and clear. I am a generous man. You remember the chest you saw in my upstairs office. Half of that can be yours. Sign the papers. I have them here. Mr. Buchanan can still be released. My man, here, can tell the judge that he was mistaken in identifying George Shue's killer. I can see to it that no charges are brought against Deputy Holroyd, as well. Believe me. I have the connections to make good that promise."

The room fell dead silent, so still that the distant murmur of men's voices outside penetrated the thick walls of the house. Margaret stared at Pilgrim with a combination of horror and fear. "You would do all that?"

"It's a lie," Buchanan broke in. "Don't give him what he wants. He'll only double-cross you—see us dead or jailed anyway—and you'll end up with nothing. Worse than nothing!"

"Fool!" Pilgrim flared. "This is your only chance!"

Buchanan eased himself imperceptibly straighter on the floor. He could still feel the revolver hidden in the back of his belt, hard against his spine. He could reach it and take out both Enderly and Slater. He knew that.

But Pilgrim still had Margaret crushed against him. There was no way Buchanan could fire at him.

"The paper is on the desk, here," Pilgrim told Margaret softly, nudging her toward a small desk against the wall by the windows. "Sign it! Don't be as big a fool as he is!"

Margaret resisted being pushed toward the desk. "No!"

Pilgrim twisted her arm higher. *"Sign,* damn you, woman! Don't you see I've done everything I can to allow you a way out of this? Don't you see how I feel about you? Under other circumstances—"

Margaret tried harder to pull away. With a muffled oath, he levered her captive arm with savage force, drawing a broken cry from her.

Buchanan couldn't stand it. He went for the gun hidden in his belt.

At the same instant, Margaret's free hand made a swooping movement toward the sash of her dress. Her hand seized something—light glittered on bright metal—and she struck at Pilgrim's face.

Pilgrim screamed and staggered backward. Blood fountained from his left eye, which now had a pair of short-handled scissors embedded deep in the socket.

Margaret was released and fell free to the floor.

Buchanan had the gun out. Both Enderly and Slater went for their revolvers. Buchanan's first shot hit Enderly in the face, spraying red and bone chips all over the wall behind him. Slater fired, but his shot hit the chandelier, sending showers of broken crystal everywhere. Buchanan's second and third shots buckled him over, dead before he hit the floor.

Pilgrim, like a fatally wounded elephant, lurched toward Buchanan, his small pistol aimed. Buchanan fired just in time. His first shot spun Pilgrim sideways. The next one drove him backward as if he had been kicked by a horse. The huge man crashed into the windows and burst through them in a cascade of glass.

The door slammed open. Two of Pilgrim's men rushed in. Holroyd, one of the fallen men's guns in hand, opened fire. His first shot drove the first man into the second, and Holroyd blasted the second one just as Buchanan fired his last round into both of them as they tangled and slammed to the floor.

Outside, men were yelling and running.

Holroyd, his face so pale it seemed ablaze with

its own light, stepped into the doorway and fired once more, into the porch roof. *"Hold it!"* he shouted in a voice that split the night.

There was a sudden partial break in the shouting, the feet on the porch stopping in their tracks.

Into the sudden relative silence Holroyd called sharply, "I'm the law here! Everything is under control! *Abercrombie!* Get up here to the house! It's over!"

Buchanan held his breath. Holroyd might be blasted at any instant, and the mob might take over.

But in the confusion, the deputy marshal's voice carried an unmistakable ring of clear authority. There was no answering angry shout, no attack. Holroyd's strength had stopped them in their tracks.

Behind Buchanan, Margaret sobbed. He turned and hurried to take her in his arms just as she collapsed.

TWENTY-THREE

One week after the death of Lucas Pilgrim, Jim Buchanan and Pat Holroyd stood with Sheriff J. D. Abercrombie in front of his Missoula jail. Steady drizzle fell, obscuring the mountains.

Abercrombie, like so many others, had long since abandoned Pilgrim's sinking empire.

"I'm mighty glad all them misunderstandings has got ironed out," Abercrombie said, stuffing tobacco in his mouth. "Why, when I think how close we come to putting you on trial, Jim, when what you done was in self-defense, I just get the shudders all over!"

Buchanan exchanged the briefest ironic glance with Holroyd. "I think we're all relieved, Sheriff."

Abercrombie turned to Holroyd. "And now that we got the case dismissed, both the judge and me hope Marshal Turner will see that it was all a misunderstanding. We sure don't need the bother or expense of a grand jury around here."

Holroyd paused to relight his wet cigarette before replying. There had been a few anxious hours after the climactic events at Pilgrim's ranch. Holroyd had moved with dramatic swiftness to assert his authority, and the confused and frightened Abercrombie had knuckled under. Now Holroyd's boss had arrived from Helena, and Abercrombie, like other locals who had been in Pilgrim's pocket, was bending over backwards to make sure he couldn't be accused of conspiracy or corruption in office.

With Pilgrim's prime enforcers dead along with him, his tight control over an empire had crumbled overnight. The ranch and mining operations were stumbling along under Jepton Laird, the nearest thing to a business manager that Pilgrim had had. A handful of previously unknown investment partners had come out of the woodwork, and a huge court battle seemed likely over division of the estate.

No one wanted to admit he had ever been a Pilgrim ally. Into the business leadership vacuum, a half-dozen would-be local entrepreneurs had appeared to try to assume leadership and influence. Missoula and its environs were in for an interesting and stormy period of stress and change.

Holroyd told Abercrombie, "I guess time will tell about a grand jury, Sheriff."

"Well," Abercrombie said, and spat brown juice into the mud, "any way I can be of assistance. Any way at all. You savvy?"

"I savvy," Holroyd said with a smile, and turned away with Buchanan to walk up the street in the direction of the hospital.

"I never saw anybody turn around so fast," Buchanan said. He was still a little dazed by how quickly Pilgrim's shadow had dissipated, how easily the trumped-up murder charges and everything else had been sluffed off. "He's scared to death of a grand jury."

"He ought to be," Holroyd said. "Corrupt bastard."

They crossed an intersecting street. The drizzle got heavier, and Buchanan lowered the brim of his

Stetson against it. "Is Marshal Turner going to let Mrs. Devine keep on running the house out there?"

"For now," Holroyd told him. "There's nobody else. And somebody is needed. With the hard cases all dead or run off, she's as good an overseer for the regular ranch operations as anybody could find."

"She probably saved us, leaving those scissors in the sewing."

"I know," Holroyd agreed grimly.

"We were damned lucky, friend."

"Tell me about it."

"And the arm is getting better all the time?"

Holroyd flexed it slightly inside the sling. "Yep."

"You need to go slow. Let it heal."

"Tell me about *that*."

They reached another intersection, one in front of a drygoods store, and stopped a moment.

"To think," Holroyd said, "that Pilgrim had a million-dollar empire; but he had to have *everything*."

"From the rumors I've heard, his mines were losing heavily. He owed a lot, and he didn't have much cash left. He was getting desperate. I think he had to have that sapphire mine to get back on his feet."

"But," Holroyd pointed out thoughtfully, "the sapphire mine might never be."

"People will look harder out there now."

"But that crazy old mountain man had searched for half his life, hiding his first find for fear somebody would jump his claim. And he never found another vein."

"Maybe there isn't another vein," Buchanan suggested.

"So the old man lived and died hiding a chest that was *all there was?*"

"Maybe," Buchanan said.

"God. Of course there were always rumors about old Eb Craddock. Some said he was rich, some said he knew where there was a golden mountain. But most just thought he was insane, sitting out there all alone, shooting at trespassers."

"He must have thought he was close to a fortune like nobody had ever seen before. And Pilgrim must have heard the stories, and believed them enough to have him watched."

Holroyd smacked the palm of his hand against his own forehead in a gesture of sudden insight. "Then the old man died, and Shue followed Joe Ford."

"Yes. And saw him drag something out of the water, and shot him to get it."

"The chest just made Pilgrim all the more sure that there was a treasure of a lifetime out there someplace."

Buchanan nodded again. "But it's like I said. Maybe there never was any more treasure. Maybe poor Joe was killed for a mirage. And all of this didn't have to be."

"Damn! If Pilgrim hadn't been so greedy, hadn't wanted so bad to have it all—"

"Then he wouldn't have been Pilgrim, would he?"

Holroyd had no answer for that. He faced Buchanan and silently offered his hand. The two men looked at each other. Lines of strain and tension were etched in both their faces, and it would be a long time before these wore off. The coming weeks would see more complications and confusion, and their faces reflected that knowledge, too.

But after staring at each other for a long minute, they both grinned. Holroyd turned and limped north. Buchanan went south.

Sister Immaculata met Buchanan in the visitors' room. Her smile was sunny and genuine. "You're late today!"

"Five minutes," Buchanan admitted.

"She's already asked about you twice."

The bantering comment filled him with joy. Despite all the horror she had been through, Margaret had never fully yielded again to the darkness threatening her mind. Two days ago she had signed a land sales contract with Ansonia Mining of Butte for twenty-five thousand dollars. It was anybody's guess whether she would ever win full claim to the steel box of sapphires now deep in the county's vault; the basis of her claim was fragile at best, the lawyer Hammond had told them, and the litigation might drag on for years. In the meantime, the land payoff was more than she had ever imagined she would have, and her sale to Ansonia had retained ten percent of the mineral rights. If the sapphires had come from her property, or if sapphires were found there, she would have a continuing good income.

All the good news had been more healing to her than a magic balm. Her insistent complaints about the timing of Buchanan's visits was just one measure of her growing mental health.

"Shall I take you back to her room?" Sister Immaculata asked now.

"I think I can find it," Buchanan told her.

"I suspect you can at that," Sister said mildly, and turned away.

Going back down the corridor, Buchanan found Margaret with her head bowed over a book. Hearing his footfall, she dropped the book and stood, her eyes big with pleasure and love. Her dress was starkly simple, long sleeves and high neck with no ornamentation, but she didn't need any ornamentation.

"Hi," she said softly.

"You look even better than yesterday," he told her after their brief embrace.

"I *am* better than yesterday!"

They stared at one another with gladness.

She said, "And now the last legal problems are over for you?"

"Yes."

"And you're really a free man."

"Yes, and it feels good."

She turned from him and walked to the window. "What now?"

"Now?" He didn't understand.

"Will you be leaving Missoula?"

"I don't know. Not yet." He was confused. "I wrote Joe's family. I don't need to hurry back to tell them anything."

She turned to face him, her expression unreadable. "Then you'll stay a while?"

He blurted, "As long as you'll let me."

"I've been thinking about that."

She stopped, then, and he held his breath. *What was she driving at?* He simply looked at her, loving her.

She told him, "I'll be here weeks yet. Maybe months."

"I understand."

"And," she added, "I want you to stay with me."

252

"Then I will," he said immediately.

"And when I go," she added, "I want you to go with me."

"Does that mean," he asked slowly, "what it sounds like?"

"Oh yes," she said very softly, very lovingly. "It most certainly does—if it sounds like I hope you'll put up with me through all the time it might take for me to get really, really well again." Her eyes changed and her brave tone faltered. "If it sounds like—I love you."

In her front office, Sister Immaculata finished brewing fresh tea, and carried the tray with the pot and two pretty porcelain cups back to Margaret's room. She thought it would be nice for Margaret and Mr. Buchanan to have tea while they visited on such a dreary day.

When she reached the open door of Margaret's room and glanced in, however, she stopped very abruptly. The two young people embracing in front of the rain-wet window did not need tea right now. As a matter of fact, they didn't look like they needed anything, except one another, and time.

Smiling to herself, Sister Immaculata tiptoed back up the hall to the front of the building and drank the tea herself, humming as she did so.

THE DESTROYER by Warren Murphy & Richard Sapir

EDGE by George G. Gilman

#5 BLOOD ON SILVER   (17-225, $3.50)
The Comstock Lode was one of the richest silver strikes the
world had ever seen. So Edge was there. So was the Tabor
gang — sadistic killers led by a renegade Quaker. The volup-
tuous Adele Firman, a band of brutal Shoshone Indians,
and an African giant were there, too. Too bad. They
learned that gold may be warm but silver is death. They
didn't live to forget Edge.

#6 RED RIVER   (17-226, $3.50)
In jail for a killing he didn't commit, Edge is puzzled by
the prisoner in the next cell. Where had they met before?
Was it at Shiloh, or in the horror of Andersonville?

This is the sequel to KILLER'S BREED, an earlier volume
in this series. We revisit the bloody days of the Civil War
and incredible scenes of cruelty and violence as our young
nation splits wide open, blue armies versus gray armies,
tainting the land with a river of blood. And Edge was
there.

*Available wherever paperbacks are sold, or order direct from the
Publisher. Send cover price plus 50¢ per copy for mailing and
handling to Pinnacle Books, Dept.17-494, 475 Park Avenue
South, New York, N.Y. 10016. Residents of New York, New Jer-
sey and Pennsylvania must include sales tax. DO NOT SEND
CASH.*

THE EXECUTIONER
by Don Pendleton

#1:	WAR AGAINST THE MAFIA	(17-024-3, $3.50)
#2:	NIGHTMARE IN NEW YORK	(17-066-9, $3.50)
#3:	CHICAGO WIPEOUT	(17-067-7, $3.50)
#4:	VEGAS VENDETTA	(17-068-5, $3.50)
#5:	CARIBBEAN KILL	(17-069-3, $3.50)
#6:	CALIFORNIA HIT	(17-070-7, $3.50)
#7:	BOSTON BLITZ	(17-071-5, $3.50)
#8:	WASHINGTON I.O.U.	(17-172-X, $3.50)
#9:	SAN DIEGO SIEGE	(17-173-8, $3.50)
#10:	PANIC IN PHILLY	(17-174-6, $3.50)
#11:	SICILIAN SLAUGHTER	(17-175-4, $3.50)
#12:	JERSEY GUNS	(17-176-2, $3.50)
#13:	TEXAS STORM	(17-177-0, $3.50)